A Dance to
Still Music

A Dance to Still Music

Barbara Corcoran

Illustrated by Charles Robinson

AN ALADDIN BOOK
Atheneum

PUBLISHED BY ATHENEUM
COPYRIGHT © 1974 BY BARBARA CORCORAN
ALL RIGHTS RESERVED
PUBLISHED SIMULTANEOUSLY IN CANADA BY
MCCLELLAND & STEWART, LTD.
MANUFACTURED IN THE UNITED STATES OF AMERICA BY
THE MURRAY PRINTING COMPANY, FORGE VILLAGE, MASS.
ISBN 0-689-70440-2
FIRST ALADDIN EDITION

To Jeanne, *sans qui* . . .

A Dance to
Still Music

1

MARGARET POINTED TO THE SIGN THAT SAID SIX BOLLOS
twenty-five cents, and laid her quarter on the counter
of the little outdoor stall. The Cuban woman nodded
and lifted the bollos from the bubbling fat, onto waxed
paper to drain. They looked like the doughnut balls that
Margaret's mother made sometimes, or used to make
when they still lived in Maine. But the bollos were made
of smashed-up black-eyed peas and garlic, fried in deep
fat, and they were delicious.

Also Margaret liked to come here because the Cuban
woman never talked to her. Back home, people had
gotten used to her deafness; almost everyone knew her
and knew she wanted to be left alone. Down here they
didn't know. The people were friendly and they often
spoke to her. Sometimes she could read their lips a little.
She had gotten pretty good at reading lips, mostly by
watching TV and by talking to herself in front of a

mirror, but it was hard if you didn't know the people or know what they might be talking about. And some people she couldn't read at all. Her mother said it was because people in Key West had a different accent; but she couldn't always read her mother, either, especially when she talked fast.

The Cuban woman handed her the little bag of hot bollos, and she walked through Old Mallory Square, past the Conch train that was filling up with tourists for the sightseeing tour, past the gift shops and the shell shops, down to the water's edge. She sat down on a chunk of wood. A fishing boat was anchored near the shore, and a man was painting the deck. It reminded her of her grandfather. He had always been painting his boat. He'd been deaf for as long as she could remember. Deaf as a haddock, as they said in her part of Maine. One reason she avoided talking to people was that she remembered how he had yelled in a funny, hollow voice, unable to hear himself. He had embarrassed her lots of times, but no matter how often her mother or his sisters told him he was yelling, he wouldn't believe it. She'd often been irritated with him herself. And now she was deaf as a haddock and she kept her mouth shut, but it was hard. She'd always liked to talk to people.

A gull swooped past the end of the dock. She thought from his open mouth that he was squawking. Farther out, two pelicans folded their wings and dove in tandem, like rocks, their heavy bodies crashing into the water with a big splash. She wondered if they followed

(4)

the shrimp boats out to sea, the way the gulls in Maine followed fishing boats.

The sun shone warmly on her head, although it was late December. She couldn't get used to the weather. At home she would be wearing two sweaters under her coat, and mittens, boots, and everything. She took a deep breath of the soft, moist air. It was funny air, almost like a light blanket that you could snuggle up in. There was the smell of fish and salt that she was used to, though it wasn't as sharp a smell as it was at home. And all this week there had been another smell, too. At first it puzzled her; it smelled like gunpowder. But then she saw some boys shooting off firecrackers and realized they must do that to celebrate the holidays. When you couldn't ask, or just pick up information from what people said, you had to try to figure things out. And in a place so different from Maine, it wasn't always easy.

She took a pamphlet that she had found on the ground near the Chamber of Commerce out of her pocket. "Key West is Living Easy," it said. English, Cubans, people from the southern states, Bahamians, early pirates. She'd like to talk to the descendant of a pirate—that would be something. She sighed and got up, wadding up the bollo bag and finding a trash can.

She walked along the waterfront, cutting through lumberyards and marine supply yards, till she came to the pirate ship. It was a big thing, put together, the signs said, from parts of real pirate ships. Some treasure-diving outfit owned it. Yesterday she had gone up the gangplank and wandered around, after the guide had taken a group on the tour. But she'd been disappointed with the main deck. Part of it was a big curio shop, and part of it looked like somebody's house, with a raised-hearth fireplace and a bar. Still it looked good when you stood on the dock and saw all that rigging. She wondered what her grandfather would have thought of it. Not much, probably.

She jumped as someone grabbed her arm. A man with a four-by-four balanced on his shoulder was trying to get past her. She knew from the look of irritation on his face that he had told her to move. He scowled and muttered as he went by her. She was always making people mad, since she'd gotten deaf.

She started up the street toward the center of town. There was the whole afternoon to kill yet, before she could go to the restaurant for supper, the restaurant where her mother was a waitress.

She stopped at every cross street, looking carefully for cars. Just before they left Maine, she'd been almost knocked down by a motorcycle that barreled down on her. She hadn't heard him coming, of course. Missing the sounds you liked—people's voices, music, the wind, the sea—that was awful, but the scary part was all the noises you couldn't hear like car engines, horns, shouts, sirens —all the things that said "look out." She was aware of some loud noises, but she couldn't identify them or tell what direction they came from, and although she could hear some voices a little, she couldn't sort out the words.

She stubbed her toe on the broken pavement and grabbed at a big tree that grew out of the sidewalk. These sidewalks buckled and cracked as if the sea had the power to push right through the coral island in wild flings of surf. They were dangerous if you forgot to look where you were going.

She paused at the pirate museum and torture chamber, admission one dollar, and read the signs. Her mother had taken her in one day, and they'd shuddered at the guillotine and all the other devices of cruelty. For once she'd been glad she couldn't hear, so she didn't have to listen to the tape recording that described how these people tortured each other. She'd gone through a period, when she was ten or eleven, when she liked horror movies and torture and all that, but she didn't want any part of them anymore. She wouldn't have gone if her mother hadn't taken her.

Her mother didn't spend much time with her. The Key West job hadn't turned out to be nearly as glamorous as that guy Joe, traveling through Maine, had made it sound. He said he owned the restaurant, but that turned out to be just one of the lies. He knew the woman who owned it, that was all. He'd told big stories about its being a swanky restaurant, and how her mother would get to be hostess after they broke her in. It was just a big, plain restaurant, with some booths, tables and a long counter. No hostess, no swank. And everyone there worked long hours for not much pay. The tips, in the summertime, had been a lot better in Maine. Margaret's mother had tried to find Joe, but nobody knew where he'd gone. So they were stuck. It had taken all their savings to get down to Key West.

As a result her mother was in a foul mood most of the time, even more than in Maine. And she and Margaret got along even worse than they had there. At least, before the sickness and the deafness, her mother had been able to brag a little about Margaret's grades in school, and her being on the student council, and even finally her piano playing, although she'd fought that. It was Grandfather who had bought the old piano and paid for Margaret's lessons.

"He can't hear her practice," her mother used to say, with that bitter little laugh she had, to let you know how tough her life was. At the last recital Margaret played in, though, her mother had given five tickets to her friends. Now she had nothing to be proud of. In fact, Margaret suspected they'd really come to Florida to get away from all the people they knew. She was an embarrassment to her mother.

Margaret sat down on the bench in front of the post office. No good thinking about all that, or about her music that she couldn't use anymore. She knew perfectly well she hadn't been good enough ever to have a career in music. What she had done best was listen. And she missed that so much, it made her ache.

She got up, feeling tired all of a sudden. Or bored, or whatever. Nothing to do but go back to the house and lie down, maybe read awhile. Something shot past her head, and there was a tiny puff of smoke where it landed on the sidewalk. Across the street three young boys were laughing and watching her. She smelled the firecracker and almost laughed out loud. They thought they'd scared her by shooting off a firecracker right in front of her, and she had barely heard it. She gave them a *V* for Victory sign. The boys raced down the alley. Maybe they thought it was a hex sign. She wandered along the street, smelling the pleasant leather smell from the New Hope Leather Shop, and detouring down a side street to see what was behind a big fence. It turned out to be a convent.

She lingered at different exotic plants, smelling them and feeling the petals of the flowers. Not until she was deaf had she realized how much pleasure you could get from your other senses. And the flowers and trees here were really something else. Like a jungle. Orchid trees, for instance. She had never known orchids grew on trees. Banana trees. with little clusters of green bananas. Who'd ever thought bananas would grow like that? And coconut trees. She had a coconut under her bed, waiting to see what it would do. And the great, huge breadfruit tree that she could see from the street, growing in the garden that was open to the public if you had a buck to spare. And everywhere, everywhere, beautiful hibiscus, red ones, yellow ones, salmony-pink ones. She had begun to learn the names of all the odd palm trees, too, because one of the motels had signs under its trees and plants to tell you what they were. If she had a picture of herself, leaning nonchalantly against a big old wicked-looking cactus, she'd send it to the kids back home. But they'd probably say, "Who's that?" She'd been out of school for more than a year. People don't go on remembering you forever.

She was hungry again. Six bollos hadn't been a very filling lunch. But she had only twenty-five cents left, and if she went over to the restaurant before she was supposed to, her mother would be mad. Her mother was scared of the tough little Cuban woman who ran the place. She was scared she'd lose her job and be stranded down here. That no-good Joe, with his big stories. Her mother, who was supposed to be so tough, always fell for whatever these guys told her.

Waiting at the corner for the light to change, she thought of the bat she'd seen last night, when she was out for a walk, hanging upside down from the caution light. She'd stood there a long time, watching the yellow light blink on, blink off, and the bat just hanging there as if he were in the jungle or something. Well, the town was kind of like a jungle with people in it. It gave you the feeling that if people moved away for a little while, you'd never be able to tell where the city had been.

She climbed the rickety steps to the grocery store on the corner and spent her quarter on a long loaf of fresh crusty Cuban bread. Her mother said the man who ran the grocery store spoke only Spanish. Anyway, he never said anything to her. An old woman sitting on the top step, bouncing a small black-eyed baby on her knees, gave Margaret a quick sidelong glance.

Margaret walked two blocks to the street where she lived. The houses were mostly old, rundown two-story houses with porches running the width of both floors— galleries, they called them. The windows, which came to the floor, had faded green shutters that closed against the sun and the possible quick wind or rainstorm. They looked like blind eyes. The Chamber of Commerce booklet said these were Conch houses, named after the native Key Westers who were called Conchs, pro- nounced like *Conks*, because of the shellfish that was a big part of their diet. Conch steak, conch chowder, conch bean soup, and conch everything else. Her mother complained about the unfamiliar food that people or- dered. "Who ever heard of a jewfish?" she'd said, the first night she came home from work, tired out. "Who ever heard of grits and grunts? This is a crazy country." Margaret had made her write down "grits and grunts" because she thought she must have misunderstood. Maybe it wasn't any crazier than New England's red flannel hash.

Most of the houses had little designs made of tile in their yards, and lots of flowers and trees and cactus. As Margaret turned in at the weatherbeaten house where she and her mother had a tiny apartment, she reached out and touched a thorn on a crown-of-thorns plant. It pricked her finger and drew a drop of blood. How much it would hurt to have a crown of thorns jammed down on one's head. She shivered.

As she passed the landlady's room, she saw her in front of the television, watching a soap opera, leaning toward it as if she dreaded to miss a word. Margaret's mother said that Mrs. Parrish always had the sound on full blast. Margaret paused for a second. She had never paid much attention to TV; she had always had so much else to do. But now she would have given anything to have heard the loud barrage of TV voices.

She went up the narrow stairs to their apartment and went in. The beds weren't made. Her mother, who had still been asleep when Margaret left the house, must have overslept and left in a hurry; she was usually so tidy. Margaret threw herself down on her own rumpled cot and stared with distaste at the dingy little room. Next month, if she hadn't gotten the ear infection last year, she would have been starting the second half of her freshman year at the new high school. Instead she was in a strange, tropical city, in her own strange unhearing world, and nobody knew what to do with her. She couldn't imagine what would become of her. She pulled her pillow over her head, trying to shout out the constant noise that whined and roared and buzzed in her ears.

She said the word "handicapped" over to herself three or four times. She made herself do it every day, to get used to the idea. Then she lay still, knowing she would fall asleep in a minute. She had learned to fall asleep almost at will. It was a way of shutting out the terrible loneliness and fear. Almost like suicide, only it left you an option. She flung one arm wide on the narrow bed, and in a minute she was asleep.

2

SHE AWOKE WITH A JERK, CONSCIOUS THAT SOMEONE
was in the room. It was Mrs. Parrish, filling up the whole
doorway and grinning her stupid grin. Margaret glared
at her, still shocked at being startled awake. She wanted
to yell at the woman, "Why don't you knock?" But she
never spoke to anyone, let alone Mrs. Parrish, and anyway, Mrs. Parrish would only say, quite reasonably,
"You wouldn't have heard me." It seemed to Margaret
that she was at everybody's mercy. There was no way
to fend people off. You couldn't escape when you
never knew someone was coming till they loomed up in
front of you.

She watched Mrs. Parrish's fat mouth make the word,
"Okay?" She could tell from her face that she was
speaking loudly. She could hear the voice as a sound far
off, words scrambled. She nodded her head and turned
her face away. It wasn't fair, she knew, to feel so furious

with Mrs. Parrish. The woman was harmless, and besides Margaret's mother had asked her to keep an eye on Margaret. But she stared with those little, curious eyes, as if she had never seen a deaf person before, as if she were looking at a freak.

When Margaret looked again, Mrs. Parrish was gone. She got up and combed her hair, and then she sat on the bed again and ate part of the Cuban bread. It was crumbly, and she knew she was getting crumbs in her bed that would drive her crazy tonight, but she didn't have the energy to get up and get a paper towel or a plate or something. Once she'd read somewhere that in France crumbs in the bed were grounds for divorce. It seemed a reasonable law. But not one she'd ever have to cope with, since she was unlikely to get married. The last time she'd heard from Peter was when she was sick and he'd brought her a potted plant that died. He'd been so uncomfortable when he tried to talk to her and she couldn't hear him that he never came back. Michael had lasted a little longer. He'd come and played Chinese checkers with her a few times, when she was able to get out of bed. But when she'd tried to talk to him, she'd seen him wince, and she'd known she must be talking loud and harsh, the way her grandfather had. Then Michael stopped coming. Most of the kids sent get-well cards and let it go at that, though a few came to visit once or twice, trying to be kind but looking curious and uncomfortable. Only Becky had kept on coming right up to the time Margaret had left for Key West. She'd brought Margaret a book on sign language, and they'd both tried to learn it, but it got too complicated after awhile, and they'd stopped. Instead they'd communicated with the little slate Margaret's mother had gotten her. Writing something on a slate and waiting while the other person read it, erased it, and wrote an answer wasn't much of a way to talk. You had to leave out so much. She'd gotten very frustrated and impatient, and a couple of times she'd thrown the slate across the room and burst into tears. The whole thing had been awful, and she knew Becky had only come out of loyalty. They had said good-bye to each other at the end with sadness and relief.

She thought about Becky and the others all the time, trying to imagine what they were doing. Sometimes she could hardly stand it not to be there. She brushed the crumbs off the bed as best she could. That Cuban bread was awfully good. She looked in the tiny refrigerator, and found only a carton half full of skim milk, some oranges, and a few odds and ends in jars. She peeled an orange and ate it slowly. There were some really strange fruits around town—guavas, papayas, plantains, sugar apples, tamarinds, soursop. She'd bought some papayas, which were good, and some plantains, which looked like big bananas but tasted awful. After she'd thrown them away, her mother said that you were supposed to cook them. Her mother was mad because she'd bought them and said she shouldn't throw away money on food when she could eat free at the restaurant. It was part of a deal with the woman who owned the restaurant that Margaret could eat dinner there. Some days her mother was allowed to bring home things that wouldn't keep any longer, like milk or pudding. So Margaret sometimes had pudding for breakfast. It wasn't too bad, especially something called flan, which was like caramel custard. She wondered if anyone else ever ate it for breakfast. That was the kind of thing you couldn't find out when you were deaf.

Maybe she ought to get out the book on sign language and really try to learn it. She and her mother had worked out a sign system of their own. Sign language was no good, though, unless other people knew it, too. She didn't know any other deaf people, and she didn't want to. At home the doctor had mentioned sending her to a school for the deaf, but Margaret was dead set against that. If she couldn't be like other people, she'd just stay by herself.

She pulled her chair up to one of the long windows and pushed open the shutter. The flaking paint streaked her fingers with little specks of green. She could look right into the top of a palm tree. A bird flew up into the tree and turned his head this way and that. She was sure he was singing, or at least chirping. The wind that she couldn't hear moved the palm fronds. Her mother said they rustled like heavy paper. With one of the quick gusts of rage that shook her lately, she slammed the shutter and threw herself down on the bed again.

Hot tears filled her eyes. She hated the whole unfair, lousy world.

After her weeping stopped, she sat up and read the newspaper. It said it was cold up north. Lots of snow. She ached for snow, and home, but if she were there, her mother would be at the restaurant, and she'd be all alone in Grandfather's big, drafty house, looking at TV without any sound. Wondering what was happening at school. Playing the piano without hearing it. Maybe it would be worse than sitting here staring at a strange bird in a strange tree. She wished she could write to somebody and tell them about all the surprising things here, try to get her mind off herself. She thought about Becky, but why start that. Becky would feel she had to answer.

If her three great-aunts hadn't died . . . she missed them so. They were her grandfather's sisters; one was a widow and two were unmarried, and they'd all lived in the big house with her grandfather and her mother and her. Aunt Tillie, who gardened furiously all summer and hooked rugs all winter; Aunt Ethel, who taught school until she was seventy, and who always brought home piles of books for Margaret; and Aunt Jan, who kept the house and smelled of fresh cookies. They had been wonderful aunts, but now they were all dead. Everybody was dead but her mother and her. And maybe her father, but he'd disappeared before she was born, and she wasn't allowed to speak of him. Only Aunt Ethel had ever talked to her about him at all, and she hadn't

really known much. He came, he married Margaret's mother, and within six months he was gone. All Margaret had was a faded and cracked snapshot of him standing in the bow of Grandfather's boat, grinning. He was handsome.

She moved her fingers across the surface of the dressing table, fingering the notes of the piece she had played in her last recital. It had been hard, and she never had gotten it all right. She longed for a piano. Even if she couldn't tell when she made mistakes, she could play the notes and hear it in her mind; that would drive her wild with frustration, but it would be better than nothing. Her fingers ached for the feeling of the keys. But this was hardly the place for a piano, even if they could afford one. The tiny apartment was crowded already, with the two beds and the small dressing table separated by a worn curtain from the so-called living-dining area, which had a card table and two chairs for dining, and a beat-up old sofa and one chair for living. At the end were the smallest stove and refrigerator Margaret had ever seen, and a chipped sink. The bathroom was down the hall. After Grandfather's big house, it was like living in a shoe box. She hated it so much, it made her head ache to think about it. She kicked the end of the sofa and hurt her toe.

The sudden little stab of pain in her toe changed her mood. She'd spent another long day just like all the other days, killing time, waiting for night so she could go to sleep and forget the whole rotten mess she was in. She put both hands on her ponytail and pulled it back till it hurt. I can't go on like this, she decided. Something has to be done.

It was the first time she had thought "something has to be done." It made her feel better. What was it Aunt Ethel always said, "When you've got a problem, just put on your thinking cap." Okay. She'd put on her thinking cap. First of all, she'd make her mother listen to reason. Back in Maine there had been hearing aid salesmen always dropping in to the restaurant to sell her mother on a new, miraculous hearing aid for Margaret. They were always expensive. Two of them had been thrown away when they moved. Neither of them worked. Now she knew her mother had been taken in by another ad. The salesman had come by and talked to them both at the restaurant. But the doctor had said that with Margaret's type of hearing loss, he didn't think a hearing aid would help. But her mother kept hoping. She felt guilty because she hadn't paid attention when Margaret had first had a bad cold and then an earache. She'd given her some aspirin and sent her to bed. When she'd finally gotten concerned, the damage had been done. It wasn't her fault; she just hadn't realized. But she blamed herself.

So all right. No more money thrown away on hearing aids and no more having to put up with stupid, unctuous salesmen. She'd make that clear to her mother tonight. But where did that leave her? That was not doing something, and the question was what would she *do*? In her mind she went over her assets, or at least her former assets. She was a good student; she could play the piano medium well, and she could sing a little; she'd been active in school plays. Now, what could she do with those things? She sat down on the sagging sofa and thought. Nothing. She couldn't perform, she couldn't teach, she couldn't go to school . . . What did other deaf people do? She could write a book, like Helen Keller, only she didn't have anything to say, except that being deaf stinks. If you were blind, people were sorry and they helped you across the street, but if you were deaf, they were just irritated.

The only kind of life she could imagine was living all by herself somewhere, with lots of books and some animals around. Lots of cats. Maybe she could get some kittens from that bunch of cats at the Ernest Hemingway House. Those cats must really get out of hand. The pamphlet said they were descendants of his fifty cats. Some of them were beautiful calicoes. She could get some of Ernest Hemingway's calico cats and a lot of books and a dog to tell her when someone threatened her privacy. But where would she live? What would she do for money? Maybe she could pick fruit. You wouldn't have to talk to pick fruit, and somebody must hire people to pick all the fruit that grew on the island.

She felt a little better. She'd tell her mother she was going to pick fruit. And maybe at night she could be a dishwasher somewhere. Then when she'd saved up some money, she'd buy a little cabin off by herself and have a garden for food.

She got up and changed into a clean shirt and her other jeans. Aunt Ethel was right; a thinking cap was a very good thing.

3

SHE LOOKED IN THE WINDOW OF THE RESTAURANT AND decided she'd better wait a little while. Quite a few people were still eating. Her mother hadn't cared if she'd hung around the place where she worked in Maine, but of course, that was different; there they had known almost everybody who came in, and anyway that was before Margaret got deaf. After she got deaf, she never went downtown at all, except to the doctor's office.

She watched her mother for a moment, as she filled four glasses with water and carried them to a table. She was a good waitress, quick and efficient, and she joked a lot with the customers, especially the men, although she almost never joked at home. Men cheered her up.

Margaret saw her smile and say something to the two couples she was serving. The man at her elbow looked up and laughed. She said something else and wrote down their order. She was short and did toe-touching exercises every night to keep her waist down. Her hair was getting a little gray, although she was only thirty-five. She put stuff on it, but Margaret thought the gray was pretty. She had to wear glasses now, but kept taking them off because she said they drove her crazy and made her feel about a hundred years old. She had a real thing about getting old. Margaret thought it might be because she had lived so long with her father and her aunts. Aunt Tillie used to say that Maggie, as they called her, hadn't had time enough for being young. Too much responsibility too soon. Meaning me, Margaret thought. She got stuck with me and not even a husband to show for it. What would the aunts think now—poor Maggie stuck with a handicapped kid.

Margaret turned away and went up Duval Street to the big white Episcopal church. The sign said it was the oldest Episcopal church in Florida. It was very pretty. Not white wood, like most churches, but some kind of cement or something. Margaret liked to go inside when no one was around and look at the stained glass. She'd never seen a church just like it.

After a while a man came in from a door near the altar, crossed himself, and sat down at the organ. He hadn't noticed Margaret. She sat on the edge of the pew, watching his hands fly over the keyboard, wanting so much to hear the music that she could hardly bear it. When she couldn't stand it any longer, she got up quickly, losing her balance as she sometimes did since she was deaf. He looked around, and she realized she must have made a clatter. She hurried outside.

There was a bench near the sidewalk and she sat down, breathing hard as if she had been running. It wasn't fair, it wasn't fair, *it wasn't fair!* She tried to concentrate on the people going by. The streets always seemed full of people sauntering along, day and night. No one hurried. A black man in a white starched uniform rode by on a bicycle, going so slowly she wondered how he kept his balance. He had a big wire basket behind the seat, and some kind of bell on the front of the bike, bigger than an ordinary bike bell. He must sell something, fruit or something like that. He rode very straight, with great dignity, not looking at anyone. Maybe he was like those street vendors she'd read about in Charleston, who go through the streets calling "She-crab, she-crab!"

Too hungry to wait any longer, she went back to the restaurant. Most of the people were gone, and her mother was leaning on the counter with a cup of coffee in her hand. One elderly couple sat at a table near the door, and at the opposite end, three teenagers were drinking Cokes and laughing, their heads together. At home, kids would be in their houses now, having their supper.

Her mother looked up and nodded at her. Margaret sat down at the counter, near her mother but not directly in front of her. The old woman who owned the restaurant peered out of the door of her dark little office, glanced at Margaret with her shrewd, quick-moving eyes, took in the teenagers, and then disappeared again. Margaret was a little afraid of her because she was so sharp-eyed and unsmiling, but she was grateful for the fact that the woman never tried to talk to her. Except for those quick looks that acknowledged her presence, she paid no attention to Margaret at all.

Margaret's mother studied her, the way she often did nowadays. It made Margaret nervous. She could almost see the thought behind it, "what am I going to do with this albatross around my neck." Although she doubted if her mother would use that phrase, that was how she thought of herself, a big, heavy seabird, like the pelicans she saw out here; and she was hanging around her mother's neck like a terrible weight.

"Everything jake?" Her mother mouthed the words so Margaret could read her lips. "Jake" was her mother's word for okay. She had never brought her slang up to date.

Margaret nodded and looked down at the menu. Sure, everything was jake. Couldn't be jaker. She studied the menu, although she would get what her mother brought, usually the day's special. Or a hamburger if the special was gone. That was all right. The food there was pretty good, and nobody ever told her not to eat so much. In a way she was lucky to be there.

While she read the menu that she already knew by heart, her mother brought her plate. Margaret raised her eyebrows in a question, and her mother pointed to the menu special, *picadillo*. There was rice, too. Margaret tried the *picadillo*, looked at her mother, and nodded approval. Her mother made a face. The *picadillo* was kind of a hamburger stew, only not really wet enough for a stew. It had onions, tomatoes, green pepper, olives, and raisins in it. Garlic, too, she decided. It was very good. She ate it quickly and drank the milk her mother brought.

She straightened up, feeling better. Her mother pointed to the slices of pie under the big lucite cover, and Margaret indicated the Key lime pie. She loved it, but usually it was all gone by the time she ate. Her mother gave her a little smile, knowing how she felt about the Key lime pie. She seemed in a good mood to-night. Often she was all scowls and weariness.

Margaret glanced in the mirror that ran along the wall in front of her. The teenagers were still there. One boy and the girl were sitting with their arms around each other. The other, a tall, dark, good-looking boy, looked up and caught Margaret's eye in the mirror. He smiled. She looked away at once.

When she looked again, he was staring absently at the straw in his hands, folding it and refolding it in little wet pieces. For the moment he seemed to have forgotten the others. He tapped his foot constantly, as if he heard some tune in his head. Margaret looked at the jukebox to see if it was playing, but it wasn't lighted up. He caught her eye again, and again he smiled. It was a nice smile. But she frowned and made a production out of

finishing her pie, giving every bite careful attention. In Maine—before—it had been fun to hang around the Dairy Queen or the pizza parlor with the kids. A lot of talk about nothing special—jokes and wisecracks. All the little filigrees of conversation that she never got anymore.

In a minute her mother came from behind the counter and went to the cash register by the door. The teenagers were leaving. As they paid and went out, the tall boy looked back, and then came toward Margaret. She didn't look at him, but she knew he was saying something to her. Her cheeks burned. And then in the mirror she saw her mother come up to the boy and speak to him. His expression changed, first to surprise, and then to that look she knew so well, of mixed embarrassment and pity. He left quickly.

Margaret's mother put her hand on Margaret's shoulder for a second, but Margaret shrugged it off. She knew just what her mother was thinking because she'd said it a thousand times: "Just say to people, 'I'm sorry, I can't hear.' " As simple as that. She should say, in her loud, hoarse voice that would sound like a Maine foghorn, "Buzz off, friend. I'm a handicapped person." What was it the blind called themselves? Non-sighted? Something like that. She could say, "I happen to be non-heared." Non-heared? Non-listening? There wasn't any comparable word that she could think of. She'd just have to say, "Shove off. I'm deaf as a haddock."

Her mother and the owner sat down at the long table at

the far end of the restaurant. They were drinking coffee and talking. Now and then they glanced at her. "What to do with that kid of mine," her mother was probably saying. What to do, what to do. She swung her stool around and got down.

At the door she met Big Ed Smith her mother's latest admirer. There were always admirers, but as far as Margaret knew, no proposals. Not too many guys wanted to marry a thirty-five-year-old woman with a fourteen-year-old kid. And certainly not with a problem kid. Her mother would never get a husband as long as she was around.

Big Ed touched the yachting cap that he always wore on the back of his head and gave her a big, phony grin. She didn't like him. Her mother said he'd told her about a school for deaf kids in St. Augustine. Margaret knew he would like her out of the way. Maybe he wanted to move in with her mother.

Margaret wrinkled her nose as he went past. Big Ed always smelled of fish. He was a retired Navy man, who had come back here and bought a couple of shrimp boats. They were manned by hired crews, so he went out himself only when he felt like it. He always had a big wad of bills in his pocket.

Margaret looked back and saw her mother's face light up as Big Ed sat down beside her. Even the owner smiled. Big Ed ate most of his meals here, and he was a good tipper.

Outside on the darkening street, Margaret hurried to

(*31*)

the apartment. Tourists sauntered past her, sometimes smiling and saying hello. She nodded and hurried on. Outside the music store two young black men were doing a little tap dance. She glanced up at the loud-speaker over the door and realized it must be playing. She felt as if she were walking inside a thick cocoon, where no sound could reach. Sometimes she felt as if she didn't exist at all.

At home she undressed quickly in the dark, got into her rumpled bed, and fell asleep.

4

AS USUAL, HER MOTHER WAS STILL SLEEPING WHEN Margaret got up. A note on the table said, "Flan in frig." She ate the custard and took an orange with her, and a pencil and some paper.

It was still early. She walked out to the beach, the one they said was the southernmost point in the United States, and sat down on the pilings of the pier, just beyond the sign that said DANGER: KEEP OFF! High winds had badly damaged the pier. Not much of it was left now except the pilings, some of them leaning at crazy angles, and a few of the planks that had originally covered it.

The gulls soared and dipped; and the pelicans flapped down and staggered upward. Farther out, a frigate bird, with his long cleft tail, flew low over the water. On the beach a tall white heron with greenish-yellow legs poked around in the sand, and then flew off.

Margaret spread out a piece of paper on the plank beside her and wrote carefully:

I am looking for a job as a fruit picker. I was ill and lost my hearing, but I am a strong worker. Thank you.

Margaret Gallagher

She read it over critically, and then added:

Or dishwashing. I am experienced.

She folded it neatly and put it in her shirt pocket. It was too early to go to the employment office.

Because it made her nervous to think about going there and having to expose herself to questions, she scrambled down off the pier and walked up and down the beach, looking for shells. She already had a pretty good collection, although the only one she recognized was the big conch. If she were still in school up home, she could give a really swinging report on shells and birds and things. But she wasn't.

She sat down on the cool damp sand and peeled her orange, wondering if you'd have to have a ladder to pick fruit. It didn't seem likely. One of the things that struck her about the Keys was how low most of the trees were, compared to the tall pines of Maine. You could just about reach the top of most of the trees she had seen, especially if you had one of those wire things on a hook.

(*34*)

Finally, when her watch said ten of nine, she walked back toward town. She stopped at a sidewalk phone booth to look up the address of the employment agency, and then checked it on the little map that you could pick up free at the restaurant.

She got to the employment agency a couple of minutes before nine. There were some people inside, but the door was still locked. In a minute an oldish man in overalls came up and tried the door. He shrugged and grinned and said something to her. She nodded and looked away. You got so you could kind of guess what people might be saying. Although she remembered the time her grandfather thought Aunt Ethel had said, "Are you going lobstering?" just because he'd expected her to say that. Instead, she'd said, "Do you have some clothes to be washed?" And he'd hollered back at her, "Might, if it don't make up to a nor'easter." He had joined the others in laughing, when they made it clear to him, but he'd felt foolish. Margaret dreaded making a fool of herself.

Someone inside unlocked the door and opened it. The man stood back politely for Margaret to go in first. She almost panicked when she saw the long counter, the files and typewriters, the woman looking at her questioningly. But it was now or never. She took the piece of paper out of her pocket and laid it on the counter in front of the woman.

The woman adjusted the glasses that she wore around her neck on a long black cord, read the note, and for a moment didn't look up. When she did, her eyes were kind. Margaret watched her, half belligerent, expecting the look of pity that she hated. But the woman looked back at the note, and then wrote, "Can you read lips?"

Margaret wrote, "Some."

The woman spoke slowly, to make it easy for her. "I'm sorry. No openings for fruit pickers. We did have a dishwashing job but it was filled yesterday."

"What?" Margaret had missed part of it. The woman wrote it down.

Margaret wrote, "Okay. Thank you."

The woman put out her hand to detain her. "Name and address? Something might come up. Something— might—come—up."

Margaret hesitated.

"How old are you?" When Margaret didn't answer, she repeated. "Age? School?"

Quickly Margaret wrote "Sixteen."

The woman looked unbelieving, but she said, "Wait." She turned away and went to a glassed-in cubicle at the back, where an older woman sat at a desk. She spoke to the woman, and they both looked in Margaret's direction.

School. They were going to check up on why she wasn't in school. Her mother worried about that, because it was the law that you had to be in some kind of school. In a minute they'd find out who she was and who her mother was, and they'd report her to the board of education. She turned and fled.

She walked fast, almost at a run, up Simonton Street, past all the little motels with their masses of flowering plants and trees, and their swimming pools with people sunning beside them and kids splashing in the water. Why hadn't she just said yes to the question about school? After all, it was Christmas vacation. Nobody was actually in school now. But she knew there would have been too many questions, too much checking up. She was crazy to think she could just walk in and get a job. But where did that leave her? What was going to happen to her? Would she never be able to get a job, be a normal person?

A police car cruised slowly up the street. For an instant she wondered if the man were looking for her. He stopped his car and got out. At the intersection another cop stood in the street, directing cars away from that area. Curious, she stopped to see what was up.

In a few minutes a gaily decorated open truck came slowly along. It was full of men and women and children in costumes. The men and boys wore ruffled shirts with red bandannas and tight black pants, and the women and girls wore vivid full-skirted dresses. Two men in the truck were playing steel drums, and everyone seemed to be singing.

Behind the truck another costumed group danced in the street. People stopped to watch, and some of them joined in the singing. Margaret leaned against a telephone pole, watching them. It was like some big pantomime, all very gay. She wanted terribly to hear it.

Suddenly a young man darted over to her and pulled her into the street. He was laughing and singing, the ends of his red bandanna flopping as he danced. He was trying to get her to dance with him. She was startled and tried to pull free, but his hands held hers tightly. Not wanting to make a fuss, she tried to dance along with him. People were smiling and calling to her. For a minute it worked, and she had a wonderful feeling of letting herself go for the first time in a long time. But she couldn't hear the drumbeat and the singing, and she lost the rhythm. She stumbled. He laughed and helped her, but when she tripped again and almost fell, he let go of her hands. She bumped against a man, a tourist in a bright flowered shirt, who yelled something to her. She yelled back, furious. "Deaf! Deaf!" She realized how wild she must have looked, when the man threw a startled look at his wife and they moved quickly away. Jostled aside by the dancers coming along behind her, she pushed her way through the crowd and sat down on a bench, out of breath. The truck and the dancers passed out of sight, and the onlookers moved away. She remembered that it was New Year's Eve.

5

WHEN SHE GOT HOME, SHE FOUND A NOTE FROM HER
mother. "Restaurant closes at five for holiday. I'm going
out with Ed, but will come home first. Have news."

Have news. Margaret read it over several times, as if
she might discover a clue. She had a sense of dread. For
the last year or so, any kind of news had turned out to be
bad.

She made lunch from the last of the Cuban bread and
some peanut butter in the bottom of a restaurant-sized
jar. Then she put on her bathing suit under her jeans and
shirt, and went to the beach. There were quite a few
people there. A holiday crowd had filled the motels. She
walked partway out on the pier that said DANGER, and
let herself down into the water. It was almost as warm
as the air. She swam straight out for some time.

When she began to get tired, she flipped over on her
back, lifting with the gentle swell. Drowning would be

a pretty good way to die, actually. Nice and clean and quick.

Last New Year's Eve she had been in the hospital with her head all bandaged up, recovering from the second surgery. She could still hear a little then, and the night nurse had come in to wish her a happy new year. The town clock had been striking midnight, a muffled sound as if it were foggy. She remembered counting the strokes. *Doom, doom, doom* . . . that's how it had sounded.

The year before that, she, Becky, Peter and some of the other kids had gone skating at Brett's Pond. They'd built a big fire on the ice, and the kids had looked like black birds, swooping in the firelight. Afterward, just before midnight, they had gone back to Margaret's house, and Aunt Jan had made them cocoa and toasted cheese sandwiches. Three months later, Aunt Jan, the last of the aunts, was dead, and before the year was out, Margaret had gotten the terrible cold that led to the earaches.

She began to swim slowly back toward the beach. She'd probably never again have such a good New Year's Eve as that one.

She sat on the sand hugging her knees, shivering a little. The sun had gone in, and the breeze was stronger. She shook the water out of her left ear. She wasn't supposed to swim without those stupid rubber ear plugs, but she couldn't see what difference it made now. She didn't even wear a cap. Dr. Hansbury would have a fit if he knew what she was doing.

She pulled on her jeans and shirt over her damp bathing suit. Maybe her mother would be home by the time she got there, and she would find out what the big news was. Probably something like she'd been fired. Or Joe had turned up with another million-dollar proposition. Her mother acted so tough and worldly, but she always trusted these characters.

Margaret walked slowly, in no hurry to get back to the dreary apartment. She stopped, for the dozenth time, to read the signs under the trees in front of one of the motels and noticed the sign by the night-blooming cereus. Right now it was just a big old ugly cactus, but the sign said it blossomed once or twice a year, with a big white flower you could smell a hundred feet away. How far was a hundred feet? She scuffed along the sidewalk, counting out a hundred steps. She looked at her feet, trying to figure how long they were. Anyway, that would be a long way to smell a flower. She wondered if she would still be around when it bloomed. Still be scuffing along the sidewalk in a wet bathing suit with nothing better to do than count out a hundred feet.

She shuddered and crossed the street. After the holiday she really would see about getting a library card. She'd gone to the library a couple of times and then panicked because she knew they'd ask what school she went to. She'd just have to name one of the high schools. They'd probably never check. She had read, several times over, the few books her mother had let her bring, and she had read and reread the three paperbacks her mother had let her buy. She could quote whole pages from *The Changeling* and she knew what Huckleberry Finn was going to do before Huck thought of it himself. She read the newspaper clear through every day, and she read cereal boxes, even matchbooks.

At the apartment, her mother had not yet come from the restaurant. It was still only a few minutes before five. Margaret lay down on her back on the floor of the gallery and stared up at the sky. The sun was out again, but there were a few stretched-out clouds drifting along on the wind. She used to look at clouds and think it would be nice to be as free as that. Now, in a way, she was; no school to go to, nothing special she had to do. And it was horrible. Being free wasn't any good unless you were free to do something or be something; no big charge in being free to be nothing.

She jumped when her mother appeared in the doorway. It was impossible to get used to people suddenly looming up. Her mother waved, and beckoned her in, looking pleased about something.

Margaret got up and went inside, nodding when her mother said, "Hi." It irritated her mother that Margaret wouldn't talk to her. "After all, I'm your mother," she'd said a hundred times. "What if you do yell a little? I don't care." But Margaret cared. If she was going to remember not to talk to other people, she'd have to remember not to talk at all. Anyway, it was too shameful to think of her voice sounding like a squawking gull, even just to her mother. She picked up the slate and wrote, "What's up?"

Her mother gave her a quick look, a strange look that Margaret couldn't quite figure out. Almost as if she were nervous about what she had to tell her. That was odd. Usually she just said what she had to say, whether it was plans or whatever, and Margaret could just, as her mother said, "like it or lump it."

Margaret sat down on the edge of her narrow bed and waited for whatever it was. Her mother pulled one of the two chairs around and sat down, facing her, with her face to the light so Margaret could read her speech. She didn't speak for a minute.

"I got me a proposal of marriage," she said finally. "Marriage."

Margaret thought she had misunderstood. She made the shape of "what?" with her mouth.

"I'm going to get married."

Margaret gasped and stared at her mother.

"Well, aren't you going to say something?" Impatiently her mother picked up the slate and shoved it at her.

Margaret looked at it for a moment. Then she wrote, "Who?"

"Ed. Who else?"

Margaret couldn't believe it. A lot of men had hung around from time to time, but there had never been any question of her mother's marrying any of them. It had never occurred to her that it might really happen. Sometimes people had said, "Maggie, you should get a husband," and Aunt Jan, who had been married once, had said she should; but to Margaret it had just been something people said, like Peter used to say he was going to live in Tahiti and eat coconuts.

Her mother looked angry. "Can't you say you're glad? You stare like it's something terrible."

Confused, Margaret frowned and shook her head.

Then as Margaret reached for the slate, her mother snatched it away. "*Say* something for once. You act like a dummy. Nobody even believes you can talk." Her face flushed with anger. She said something else, but her mouth was tight and Margaret couldn't read it. "Stubborn. Mean. Never to say a word. You want to punish me. You blame me."

Margaret opened her mouth and said, "Mother."

Her mother stared at her. "That's better."

Margaret tried again, but she couldn't bring herself to talk. She had gone too long, and she was too upset. She picked up the slate and wrote, "Hope you'll be happy."

Her mother looked at it in silence. Then she shrugged and spoke more quietly, and Margaret got some of it. "Worked and slaved . . . other people . . . all my life. Now for a change . . . a diamond. Never had a ring." She wrote it down. "I never had even a dime-store ring." She looked down at her square, short-fingered hand. "A whole karat."

Margaret wrote, "Nice."

"Nice," her mother said. "Yeah." She looked up suddenly at Margaret and spoke distinctly. "Ed likes you." She paused. "You aren't going to make a fuss, are you?" More slowly she repeated: "No fuss?"

Margaret shook her head. She was frightened. What would become of her?

Her mother stood up and walked around the room, then came back and stood in front of Margaret. "Real good school. Good school." As Margaret stiffened, she talked faster, so fast it was hard for Margaret to follow her. "Private. He'll pay for it. Come to see you often." She grabbed the slate and scribbled. "Only thing to do. Done everything I know how." She smiled nervously and spoke again. "You'll like it. Lots of kids . . . learn handicrafts—" she gestured with her hands. "Leather, weaving . . ." When Margaret didn't answer, her face grew angry again. "Don't stare at me like I'm . . . cost Ed a lot of money . . . gratitude."

"I can't go to one of those schools."

"Why not?"

How could she tell her? She couldn't write "because I was popular—I played in the orchestra. I was an honor student."

Her mother flared up. "All right. I won't marry him. I'll go right on—" She turned away, and Margaret lost the rest.

Margaret got up and went out into the gallery. She sat down on the floor and bounced a small rubber ball that

(45)

had been left out there. Bouncing it with the palm of her hand, counting the number of times she could do it without missing, she concentrated on it as hard as she could. It reminded her of Aunt Tillie, who used to play jacks with her.

Aunt Tillie would have been pleased that her mother had a chance to get married. All the aunts would. It was true that she had worked hard for other people. Margaret was really glad for her that she was marrying somebody and she'd have a real diamond and not have to work. Of course, there was no question of standing in her way. But she, Margaret, was not going to any school for handicapped kids. That was something she simply could not face. It wasn't only the idea of handicapped, although that was bad enough. It was that, as far as she could see, they didn't learn anything worth learning. Handicrafts were all anyone talked about. And what could you do with them? Maybe her hearing would come back all of a sudden and things would be the way they used to be.

She made herself go in to tell her mother how glad she was she was getting married, but her mother had gone down the hall to take a shower. Margaret went out and walked around the block a few times. She walked fast, counting her footsteps, trying to get away from the racket in her head. It was worse when she was upset. She counted carefully. She'd never considered before how many steps it would take to walk around the block.

When she came back, her mother was all dressed up

and Big Ed was standing in the middle of the apartment, practically filling it up. He was wearing a suit, with a shirt and tie, and looked as if he were going to church. He wheeled around with a big grin when Margaret came in.

"Hi," he said, and added something more that Margaret didn't get.

He never waited for an answer anyway.

When he began to talk again, all she saw was the word "daddy." He laughed and reached out a big arm, but she slid out of reach, feeling sick.

He pulled some bills out of his pocket and shoved them into her shirt pocket.

Margaret's mother shook her head and said something to him. They're talking about me, Margaret thought, and I might as well not be here. They have no right to say things about me that I can't hear. She jerked the money out of her pocket and thrust it at him, but he moved back, holding up his hands.

"No, no, no." He picked up the slate. "Happy New Year. Tie one on." He was laughing. "Get new dress," he wrote in his scrawly big handwriting.

"Ed," her mother said.

He grabbed her arm, then talking and laughing, steered her toward the door.

Margaret's mother said something to her, but Margaret didn't get it. Ed swirled her out of the apartment.

When they had gone, Margaret closed the door and threw herself on the bed. She felt as if she had a block of

(*48*)

ice inside her. Not even able to cry, she lay there till it was dark. "Thinking cap," she said aloud finally, and got up and turned on the overhead light. The pad of writing paper and her ball-point pen were what she needed. "Dear Becky," she wrote, then sat still, chewing the end of the pen, staring unseeingly across the room. Something had to be done. She had to get out.

6

Dear Becky,

Hi. Happy New Year. It's New Year's Eve, and I thought I'd write you a letter just to say hello and how's life treating you? Would you believe it's 80 degrees here right now, and I went swimming this afternoon? Gorgeous flowers blooming all over the place. It's really a neat place. How's Michael, Peter, Linda, Miss Snow, and everybody? Gosh, it seems like ten years since I saw all of you. I might be seeing you pretty soon, though, but Becky, can I swear you to a big secret? I know I can, because remember in the fourth grade when we cut our wrists, mingled our blood and swore eternal loyalty? That was just a crazy kid stunt, but just the same it means we're loyal forever, doesn't it, and we will keep each other's secrets till doomsday, right? Well, first here's the big news. My mother is going to get married. DON'T TELL. I think she would be mad if she couldn't break the news at home herself. So don't tell. Anyway, she's marrying this guy, a retired Navy man, who owns fishing boats. He's a "good catch" (get the joke?) and my mother is really happy. She won't have to work anymore, that's the best part. Of course, they want me to live with them, and all that, but I read in "Dear Abby" one time where having an older child of a former marriage caused friction. I would feel terrible to cause friction, so even though they will be very disappointed, I think I'll clear out for a while. Of course, I'll come back later. Anyway, Beck, I thought I might come home and open up Grandpa's house and live there a little while, just till the newlyweds get a chance to have some time to themselves without a stepchild, you know? Ed (that's his name) gives me tons of money, but just to economize, I think I'll hitch home, so it may take awhile. Anyway, when I get there, if I could stay with you like about two nights, just till I have time to get some wood chopped and the house warmed up and all. Would that be okay? Don't tell your mother yet. We'll surprise her. But maybe you can pave the way a little, like saying "wouldn't it be nice if Margaret came for a little visit" or something, you know? Grandpa's cellar is still full of stuff we canned, and as soon as it's spring, I'll start a garden. I won't turn the heat on and all that. I'll use the wood stove and the fireplaces. Like a pioneer lady, huh? You come over often, and I'll cook hot dogs in the fireplace, and we'll toast marshmallows. Remember New Year's Eve two years ago, at my house? I wish the aunts were still there . . .

Margaret put her head down on her arm and began to cry. But after a few minutes she mopped her face impatiently and finished the letter.

. . . so I thought I'd better warn you I may be showing up one of these days. Wouldn't want you to drop dead from surprise. Remember, keep the SECRET.

Love,
Margaret

She found an envelope and an airmail stamp. It was the only solution she could think of. The idea of hitchhiking to Maine terrified her, but what else was there? She had to save her money. She might have to buy some warm clothes on the way. It was cold up North and she didn't have any warm clothes here. Once she got there, she could get along. And she was pretty sure her mother wouldn't go to all the bother and expense of bringing her back here. What they really wanted was to get her off their hands. And she didn't blame them one bit. So okay, that was it.

She got out the old denim book bag with the drawstring that Aunt Tillie had made her. Travel light. She put in her toothbrush, a comb, pajamas, clean under-wear, a sweater, a clean shirt, pencil and paper, and *Huck Finn*. She was still wearing her bathing suit under her clothes, so she'd just leave it on.

She went out onto the gallery and looked down at the street. A lot of people were milling around, kids run-ning, cars going faster than usual. She had never really understood why people got so excited about the new year. She watched them for a while, smelling the odd mixture of salt air and flowers and firecrackers. She couldn't start out tonight. Maybe in the morning some of the tourists would be starting back to Miami. They'd be going back for the Bowl game, probably. She'd have to write out that she was hitching a ride, and she'd have to say she was deaf. She hated that idea. But there was no way around it. She opened the bag again and took out paper and pen. Carefully she printed in block letters: HITCHHIKING TO MIAMI. HOME FOR HOLIDAYS. TEMPO-RARILY DEAF FROM EAR INFECTION. THANK YOU. She looked at it critically. By the time I get to Maine, she thought, I'll probably be a very accomplished liar. She folded the paper and put it in her jeans pocket.

Without undressing, she lay down on her bed. She'd try and get some sleep now, so she could get up really early and be on her way. But she was too nervous to sleep. Her mind kept turning to possibilities. What if some kook picked her up? What if whoever picked her up reported her to the police? What if nobody picked her up?

Remembering the money Ed had given her, she took it out and counted it. She caught her breath in surprise. There were four twenty-dollar bills. If her mother knew she had all that money, she'd flip. Maybe she could take the bus partway. Except she'd need some money for warm clothes. And it might be better to save the rest to live on after she got to Maine. There were some things she'd have to buy. She folded the money carefully and put it in the small front pocket of her jeans.

She closed her eyes tight and in a little while fell asleep.

When she awoke, the room was still dark, but there was a faint lifting of the darkness outside the windows. She could see the outline of her mother in the other bed. She wondered if they'd had a good time. Her mother wasn't much of a one for drinking, but Ed usually had a beer in his hand. Probably on New Year's Eve, and the date of her engagement, her mother would have lived it up a little, too. She had it coming.

Very quietly Margaret got out of bed. Her mother didn't stir. The slate lay on the table. Margaret found the chalk and wrote:

Hi.

Thought I'd clear out and give you guys a chance. I have sensible plan. Don't worry. I'll be in touch.

M.

She wondered what her mother's reaction would be. Probably mostly relief, though her conscience would bother her. Grandfather used to say: "Maggie even feels guilty when the hens don't lay." Margaret underlined "Don't worry."

She opened the door just wide enough to let herself out. Mrs. Parrish's fifteen-watt bulb made a tiny pale dab of light at the head of the stairs. Carrying her bag in front of her, Margaret went carefully down the stairs, holding her breath as she went by Mrs. Parrish's door.

Out in the deserted street she turned in the direction of Route 1, the narrow road with its forty-two bridges that spanned the distance from Key to Key, more than a hundred miles to Miami. She walked fast, keeping in the shadows. No one was in sight. There was a lot of trash in the streets—streamers, beer cans, and spent firecrackers. A car was parked half on the sidewalk, one door still open. People would be hung over all day.

The city park and the beach across the road were littered with debris, and some couples were still stretched out on the ground, either asleep or zonked out. She walked even faster. After she reached the other side of the park and came into open country, dawn came with startling suddenness, as if someone had flipped the red-gold coin of the sun up over the dark shelf of the sea.

Ahead of her she saw a small filling station that was open. The attendant was filling the tank of an old pickup. The driver of the pickup got out and went into the station, and in a minute the attendant followed him in. Margaret moved closer to look at the pickup. It had a name on its side, a plumbing and heating company with a Miami address.

Without taking the time to think whether it was a good idea or not, she put her bag over the battered tailgate, got into the back, and crouched down. There were tools and pieces of pipe all around her. She held her breath as she saw the man come out and wave to the attendant. He got into the cab without looking back. Margaret lay as flat as she could, on top of the uncomfortable tools, hugging the side so he wouldn't see her if he looked in his rearview mirror.

She wriggled a little to get a length of pipe out from under her stomach. And if being quiet hadn't been so important, she would have giggled. She was probably going to get all the way to Miami without even having to speak to anybody, without anybody's even seeing her. If her mother should call the cops, they wouldn't be able to find anyone who knew anything about her. Nuts to you, Private School for the Handicapped; here's one handicap you won't get to fool around with.

7

IN SPITE OF THE DISCOMFORT OF THE RATTLETRAP TRUCK, she kept dozing off. She awoke with a jerk when the pickup came to a sudden, wrenching stop. It felt as if they had hit something. She didn't dare look at first, but after a minute she very cautiously raised her head. There were no other cars in sight, and at first she couldn't figure out what had happened. They were still on the highway. Then she saw the driver, near the front wheels. He was hauling something off the road. She sat up a little more to look. She couldn't see it very well, but it seemed to be a dog. He had run over a dog!

He pulled it into a marshy ditch by the side of the road. Watching it, she saw the animal's leg move. It was not dead. She was so indignant when the man left the dog and came back to the pickup, that she forgot to duck. But he didn't see her. He climbed back into the cab and revved the engine.

Margaret grabbed her bag, swung her leg over the tailgate and jumped to the ground as the pickup started off. The momentum threw her, and she fell onto the hard pavement.

By the time she was up on her feet, the pickup was already barreling along the highway, growing smaller and smaller. She went to the place where he had hauled the hurt dog.

But it wasn't a dog. It was a deer, the tiniest fawn she had ever seen. She knelt beside it. The little fawn lay on his side, staring at her with wide, frightened eyes. He shuddered when she reached out her hand to stroke him.

It must be a Key deer. She had read about them. They were a very small variety of white-tailed deer, found only in the Florida Keys. They had been almost extinct, down to about fifty deer, when the Fish and Game people took over, and made a reservation for them. She had seen the reservation sign when she and her mother had come on the bus from Miami. Poor little thing. She bent closer to see where he was hurt. He rolled his eyes, watching her, and he trembled all over. She made a little murmuring sound and touched him with the tips of her fingers. His skin twitched under her touch.

There was no blood. The problem seemed to be with one of his hind legs. The right one looked funny. The fawn struggled to get up and then fell back, panting. It was that leg, all right. If he wasn't hurt internally, maybe she could fix the leg. She'd need some kind of splint.

As she looked up, a car came along the road. It

slowed, then picked up speed again. She'd have to move the little fellow, before somebody got curious enough to stop. She knew what most people would say: "If he broke his leg, shoot him." That was what they'd said at home when Mr. Haines's Molly broke her leg. And they did shoot her.

She looked around. On their side of the road there was only a narrow stretch of beach and then the ocean. On the other side, an overgrown dirt road led off toward the Gulf. There was more cover over there. That's where they'd have to go.

He struggled as she tried to get her arms around him. He looked so wild, and his sides heaved so hard, she was afraid he'd die of a heart attack. She smoothed his side very gently, murmuring so low, she wasn't sure whether he could even hear her. Maybe she only thought she was making a sound. But he flicked his ear toward her; it seemed as if he had heard.

She knelt for what seemed a long time patting him, trying to figure out how to get him across the road without hurting him too much. And as usual, because she didn't hear people come up, she was startled when a shadow fell across the deer's haunch. Someone was standing there. She got to her feet, ready to fight off whoever it was that might want to destroy the deer. It was her deer; she had found him. And she was going to save him, no matter what.

The woman standing in front of her was short and very thin, with leathery brown skin. She wore a pair of clean white cotton slacks and a sleeveless blouse that had once had blue stripes, but was faded now almost to white. Her dark hair was cut short, and on her head was a high-crowned white Panama hat with a blue and white ribbon around it. Just behind her there was a three-wheeled bike, with a big wire basket on the back. A broom handle stuck out of the basket, and inside was a pink plastic pail full of cleaning cloths.

She was looking at Margaret with questioning eyes, and Margaret knew she had probably said something. Margaret pointed to the deer. The woman glanced at him briefly, bent over and examined his leg. She said something that Margaret didn't catch. She spoke again, and Margaret shook her head. The woman studied first Margaret, then the deer, then Margaret again.

"Can't hear?" She touched her own ears.

Margaret wished the woman would go away.

The woman bent closer. "Read lips?" She touched her own lips.

Margaret nodded.

"Okay." The woman spoke slowly; it was easy to read her lips. "Broke his leg." She pointed to the deer's leg. "Car?"

Margaret nodded again. She was braced for the woman to say, "We'll have to kill him." She didn't know how she would stop her, but she knew she would.

A car whizzed past them on the road, and the woman looked after it, shaking her head. It was obvious that she didn't like what had happened. Margaret felt a sense of relief. Maybe the woman was going to help. She bent over again and touched the fawn's leg gently. He quivered. She spoke to him, and he looked at her with his big eyes. In a moment she straightened up and looked around. She picked up a short length of branch and threw it down again. Finally she got the broom from her bike and took the ribbon off her hat. "Hold his head," she said, pointing to his head and to Margaret's hands.

Margaret held his head, warily, watching the woman. The deer trembled violently. The woman laid the broom handle along his leg, straightened the leg a little, and then swiftly bound the leg and broom together with the ribbon.

"Up." Together they got the fawn to his feet. He tried to step on the injured leg, but it gave way under him. "Easy," the woman said. She obviously had something in mind, but Margaret didn't know what it was, and she didn't know how to ask. She could only watch and be careful. The woman got her arms under the fawn and carried him to the bike. He was too big to fit in the basket, but she got his front legs in and gestured to Margaret to hold his hindquarters. She said something, but Margaret didn't get it. It was clear though that the woman knew what she was doing.

Margaret got her arm under the hind legs and braced him as the woman wheeled the bike across the road and down the dirt lane, past thickets of palmetto and short, stubby pines, and mangroves. They had to move slowly, and the woman kept looking back. The little deer made no attempt to get out. Once the woman looked at the brushy end of the broom, that stuck up in the air above the deer's haunches, and her eyes crinkled with amusement. We must really look funny, Margaret thought, but she was too busy holding the deer steady and not tripping over roots and rocks, to think much about how they looked.

Her bag, which she had slung over her shoulder, kept banging against her side, but she didn't want to let go of the deer to readjust it, so she let it bang. The fawn felt very small and light, and he stood still, although he trembled, and once or twice he turned his head and looked at her with worried eyes.

The woman turned off the dirt road, down a sloping path that was just wide enough for the bicycle. The stiff fronds of low-growing palms grazed Margaret's face.

Then the bike stopped, and Margaret peered ahead to see where they were. They had followed a path right down to the edge of the Gulf. And at the end of the path, nestled in among the mangrove roots, was a small houseboat. Moving in a quick, surefooted way, like some tropical monkey, the woman scrambled up a short rope ladder onto the boat and lowered a narrow gangplank. She ran down the gangplank and began to maneuver the bike and the deer up onto the deck of the boat.

The tilting of the bike startled the deer, and he tried to pull away, but the woman had her arm around his shoulders, and Margaret steadied him in back.

On deck, the woman said, "Wait," and disappeared into the cabin. In a minute she was back again with an old quilt under her arm and a length of narrow rope. She moved the bike forward, to the shelter of an awning, and there she spread out the quilt on the deck. With her arms under the trembling fawn, she lifted him out and stood him on the quilt, then looped the rope around his neck and tied the other end to the rail.

The fawn looked back at the broom that stuck up behind him and opened his mouth, like a lamb bleating.

"Scares him," the woman said.

She disappeared again and returned with a piece of wood and an Ace bandage. Swiftly she unwound the ribbon that held the broom, and replaced the broomstick with wood. She bound the wood and the leg together carefully with the elastic bandage.

Sitting back on her heels to look at the job she'd done, she nodded and said, "Better." Then glancing at Margaret, she stood up and ran her hand lightly along his back. "Okay, Sonny." His skin quivered, but he stood still. Turning her full attention toward Margaret then, she stood looking for a moment or two, and said, "I'm hungry." She made the motions of eating. "Are you?" Her eyes sparkled.

Margaret relaxed a little, smiled and nodded, remembering suddenly that she'd had no breakfast.

The woman unfolded an old canvas chair and set it down near the deer. She gestured to Margaret to sit down.

When she was alone, Margaret looked around. The boat was very small, squared off at both ends like a barge. The awning that shaded the deer stretched across the bow and was attached to an iron framework that had been riveted to the deck. Several canvas chairs, folded, leaned against the cabin. There were pots of geraniums all along the bow rail. She got up and moved one as the little deer stretched out his neck and nipped off a leaf. A potted banana tree and some other tropical plants that Margaret didn't recognize were placed along the frame of the cabin. The boat was spotlessly clean, and it looked freshly painted.

She walked around the cabin. On the other side, a rope hammock was swinging lightly in the breeze, and there was a big box of seashells. Some fishing gear was stowed in a long case.

Smelling food cooking, she realized again how hungry she was. She wondered if the deer were hungry. She wasn't sure what he would like. At home, deer ate bark and leaves and sometimes vegetables from the garden, when nobody was around to stop them. Alongside the boat, at the stern, so close that one of its branches leaned over the deck, a mangrove grew out of the shallow water, its network of exposed roots reaching into the Gulf like hands. She reached up and broke off part of the nearest branch and brought it to the fawn. He wrinkled his inky black nose and looked from the branch to her and back again before he ventured a dainty bite. His white-circled eyes looked even bigger than they

(65)

were, and Margaret noticed that under his chin and down the front of his throat his coat was pure white. The insides of his legs were white, too, and also under his tail. At home, she had read about the whitetail deer whose tail hairs shot up like a flag when they were alarmed. This deer had his tail down now, and she hoped that meant he was feeling safe. She wondered how old he was and how big he would get to be.

She watched him chew on the mangrove leaves. He ate slowly and thoughtfully, as if he had his mind on some big philosophical problem. Like "How am I going to get out of here?" she thought. But he didn't seem agitated now. Probably reservation deer wouldn't be as easily spooked as other deer, and down on the Keys there couldn't be too much in the way of predators, no wolves or coyotes or anything like that. She spoke to him in her mind: "You've got a pretty neat life here. You just be patient while your leg heals, and everything will be jake."

The word "jake" reminded her of her mother. She'd probably be upset at first about Margaret's leaving. But she'd soon see it was the best thing for all of them. The letter to Becky was still in Margaret's pocket. Time enough to mail it when she hit the road again. And that would have to be soon, of course. She was sorry . . . she didn't want to leave her deer. And she liked the strange little woman who was so efficient and didn't ask questions. The boat was nice, too. Maybe when she got to Maine, she could find an abandoned fishing boat to fix it up as a place to live, in the summer anyway.

She looked up and saw the woman coming onto the deck carrying a dishpan full of water. When she put the water down near the fawn, he immediately had a big, slurpy drink, lifting his head to look at them, water dripping from his chin. The woman noticed the branch of mangrove and nodded.

"Come on below." She signaled to Margaret to be careful on the very narrow stairs.

Below deck, the quarters were tiny and snug. A small round table and two captain's chairs were bolted to the floor. There was a tiny stove and a sink. Off either end of the galley, Margaret could see very small quarters with built-in bunks.

The woman nodded toward one of them, took Margaret's bag and put it on the bunk. She put her hand under her head to mean sleep and pointed to Margaret. "I sleep outside," she pointed up. "Hammock." Her gestures were quick and easy to follow. She showed Margaret where to sit at the table, and then she turned to the stove. In a few minutes Margaret had a plateful of bacon, fried eggs, and grits in front of her. It smelled so good, she thought she would float right through the ceiling. She clasped her hands together to keep from eating before the woman sat down.

"There." The woman sat opposite her and spread her napkin on her lap. She had put an enamel coffeepot and two mugs on the table, and she carefully poured the

(67)

steaming coffee. The cups had JOSIE painted on them, with a little sprig of flowers underneath. "Josie." She jabbed her thumb at her chest. "That's me."

Margaret tried not to eat fast, but in no time at all she had cleaned up her plate and Josie was filling it again. Food hadn't tasted so good since she left Maine.

They ate, Josie not speaking. It was always a relief when the other person kept still. Trying to follow what people were saying could wear you out. At last, sighing with contentment, Margaret leaned back in her chair. She made the round circle with thumb and forefinger that meant "good!" Josie smiled. She studied Margaret for a moment, and Margaret tensed up again. Now come the questions, she thought, but Josie only said, "I have to go to work. Work . . . go to work. Late . . . but okay today." She got up and found a pad and pencil and wrote: "Will you keep an eye on Sonny?"

Margaret nodded gratefully. It was exactly what she wanted. She got up to help Josie clear away the dishes, but Josie waved her away. She scraped the plates and stacked them neatly in the tiny sink. She wrote on the pad: "I clean rooms at motel. Home around two." She went into the little cabin and gave her hair three or four quick strokes with her comb.

Up on deck she pointed out some palm trees growing near the shore. They were about two or three feet tall, with long fan-shaped leaves that were silver underneath. "For Sonny." She put the broom back in the basket of her three-wheeled bike and pushed the bike down the gangplank to the path. She waved and disappeared.

Margaret thought, I am alone on a houseboat with a wounded deer, and I have a new friend. It was not at all what she had expected when she started out that New Year's morning.

8

MARGARET FOUND A MACHETE IN THE NEATLY ARRANGED cupboard in the galley, and she used it to cut big armfuls of the silver palm for Sonny. He didn't tremble anymore when she came near him, so she stood there for a minute and watched him eat. It had been kind of hard work, cutting all those palm branches, but he was enjoying them so that was all right.

"You tie into that now," she said aloud. "That'll keep you busy for a while. I'm going to clean up the galley." She looked back at him when she got to the cabin. He was still chewing and still watching her with his big velvet eyes. Sonny was something else.

She built up a little fire in the stove to heat water for the dishes, being very careful with everything. Josie kept the place so neat. Even the unwashed dishes looked clean and tidy.

She washed and polished till everything shone. The

glass that had held the milk for the coffee she washed three times, holding it up to the light of the porthole over the sink, until she could see it didn't have a streak.

When everything was spotless, she ventured into Josie's cabin because the head was on the far side of it, but she walked almost on tiptoe, feeling she was invading someone's private quarters. In there, as in the galley and the other cabin, the walls were paneled with a dark, mellow wood. A ship's clock was fastened to the wall facing Josie's bunk. Tacked to a cork bulletin board on the shelf over the built-in drawers, Margaret saw an enlarged snapshot of a good-looking young man in a Merchant Marine uniform, and a smaller picture, like the kind they take in school, of a little boy. She thought they were the same person. Next to them, on a shelf attached to the wall, were about a dozen books, mostly paperbacks, held on the shelf by a brass chain. The fittings on the doors and on the drawers were shiny brass. What would her grandfather have said to this boat? She thought he'd say, "It's a filly-lou-bird," which meant "It's a little peculiar, but I like it."

She liked it, too. It was the sort of place she'd dreamed of. Private. Away from the world. Not even radio or TV as far as she could see. She wished she could just stay there. But that was silly even to think of. No total stranger was going to take a deaf kid in and look after her. Besides, eventually even this woman was bound to ask about school or home. She wondered if it would be all right to ask if she could sleep up on the deck that night, to make sure Sonny was all right.

She went back on deck and found Sonny still munching contentedly. He had managed to lie down, his splinted leg sticking straight out. He looked at Margaret but he didn't stop chewing: She wondered if he'd like some salt; deer liked a salt lick. But that would have to wait till Josie came home. "Do you feel better?" she said to him. He flicked one ear forward. "I think you feel better." It was nice to have someone she could talk out loud to without worrying about how it sounded. She was making an effort to keep her voice very low. At any rate, she wasn't yelling, because he showed no sign of hearing a loud noise. It must be wonderful to hear all the tiniest little sounds that a deer could hear.

She put one of the canvas cushions on the deck and stretched out on her stomach to watch him. But the sun was warm and already she had put in a long day; in a minute she was sound asleep.

She woke up, with the feeling that someone was looking at her. Groggy with sleep, she raised herself up on her elbows and looked around. There was no one on deck. She was about to put her head down again when a movement on shore caught her eye. A tall woman, in ragged jeans that were too short, stood on the sand with a fishing rod and a bucket in her hand, watching Margaret. She yelled something but Margaret couldn't understand her and hoped she would just go away. The woman was wild-looking with hair that stood out like barbed wire. Margaret wanted to stare, but decided she shouldn't and sat up so she could look out to the intensely blue water of the Gulf. A high-rigged fishing boat, the kind used for big-game fishing, moved slowly up the Gulf. She watched it for a minute, and then turned to look at the shore again. The woman had moved on until she was almost out of sight in a stand of slash pine, but she was still looking back, yelling and waving her arm. It made Margaret very uneasy. If you could tell what someone was saying, then you could tell what to do. But there was no way of knowing whether the woman was just saying "hello" or "who are you?" or something, or whether she was threatening. She looked threatening.

After she had gone, Margaret slept again, and when she awoke, Sonny was chewing his cud like a contented old cow, and Josie was sitting with her back to Margaret, in a faded blue bathing suit, her high-crowned hat tilted forward over her eyes. She had a fishing pole between her knees and a bottle of beer open on the deck beside her. Her bare feet were propped up on the rail. She had swabbed down the deck around Sonny's bed. The dark stains of water were drying out.

Margaret sat up and wiped her perspiring forehead with her arm. The sun had gotten hot. As she got up and started toward Josie, Josie turned and smiled.

"Good sleep?"

Margaret smiled and nodded.

Josie pointed to another deck chair. "Coke?" She

nodded toward a styrofoam picnic cooler that was pushed back under the shade of the awning.

When Margaret was settled beside her, Josie cast her line out a little further and turned to Margaret. "Motel . . . big mess; New Year's Eve—I hate it! I used to be school . . . ." She repeated the missing word "custodian," as Margaret looked uncomprehending. "Janitor. Clean-up kid. Too old for that now." She looked at the fawn. "Sonny looks good." She turned back so Margaret could see her face. "Looks good."

Margaret watched the little deer. Now and then he snapped at a fly on his back, but most of the time he looked relaxed and peaceful. His leg must feel better, and he was not afraid of them anymore.

"By his teeth," Josie said, pointing to her own teeth, "about four months." She held up four fingers.

Margaret looked at Sonny, remembering a baby fawn she'd found in the woods in Maine once, with spots all over, like polka dots. Miss Anderson had said, in science, it was for camouflage and they outgrew the spots.

Josie got up and crouched down in front of Sonny to check the splint. She patted him.

Margaret signaled that she would be right back and went below to get her paper and pencil. She wanted to ask some things about the deer. On deck again, she wrote, "How big do they get?" Josie wrote: "Buck, sixty to ninety pounds. Does smaller." She measured with her hand. ". . . maybe two feet, two-and-a-half. All around these Keys, but hard to see except before dark or if you get up early." She had a big, clear, slanted handwriting. She finished her beer, put the bottle back on the deck, and wrote, "Were you going some place special this morning?"

Margaret shook her head and looked away. There was nothing to say. The sunlight sparkled on the bright blue water, deeper at the bow end than at the stern. It was funny how the water of the Gulf was so blue, and just on the other side of the Overseas Highway the water of the Atlantic was so green. She wondered why that was so.

Josie touched her arm to get her attention. More questions. "Hungry? Have any lunch?"

Margaret shook her head again, this time looking at Josie. She had not eaten such a big breakfast in a long time. She didn't feel hungry at all.

Speaking slowly, Josie said, "I ran away from home when I was a kid."

Margaret looked at her sharply, but Josie was looking past her, out to sea, remembering things.

"Sixteen. Ran off with a sailor. Never was sorry. Sometimes better not to be home." She paused so long that Margaret thought she had finished. But then she said, "He died—flu . . . right after my boy was born." Margaret strained to follow her. "Came back here, Danny and I; I'm an old Conch. My daddy made cigars." She held up the pencil as if to smoke it. "I talk a lot."

Margaret wrote on the pad, "Where is your son?"

(75)

"Merchant Marine." She looked at Margaret a moment. "You can talk, can't you?"

Margaret pretended she hadn't understood, and concentrated on her Coke.

Josie clamped the fishing rod between her knees and lifted her arms to stretch. "Like my boat?"

Margaret nodded enthusiastically and clasped her hands together.

"My boy made it. Danny, good boy." She said something else, but Margaret shook her head. She wished she could understand it all, but she never did, no matter how carefully the person spoke.

Josie wrote: "Danny built my boat. Always makes everything perfect." She got up and handed the fishing pole to Margaret.

Margaret held it a little nervously, hoping she wouldn't get a fish on the line and not be able to hold him. She had never done much fishing, although when she was little she had gone out with her grandfather sometimes to check the lobster pots.

In a few minutes Josie was back with two big Cuban sandwiches. She took the fishing rod back and clamped it between her knees. Margaret thought she had never had such a good sandwich. The crusty Cuban bread was spread with mayonnaise, and there were layers of sliced ham, cheese, pickle, tomato, lettuce, and potato chips. She had never heard of potato chips in a sandwich before. She touched Josie's arm, pointed to the sandwich, and made an ecstatic face.

Josie laughed. "You don't . . . words. Talking face." She pointed to Margaret's face. "Talks."

They sat comfortably in the shade of the awning, their feet on the rail, eating their sandwiches. Josie had another beer, and Margaret had another Coke. The water of the Gulf lay still, shimmering and blue. Gulls and pelicans swooped and circled and dove. Josie pointed to a white heron flying along the edge of a tangle of mangroves.

"Great white heron." She gestured toward some of the smaller Keys. "Refuge." She wrote down, "Roseate spoonbills, white-crowned pigeons. Real rare." She yawned and pushed her hat back on her curly black head.

Margaret glanced at her, beginning to worry. She didn't know whether she ought to go or not. Josie might have given her a clue that she hadn't heard. If she were going to leave, she should go now before night came. The idea of going made her feel almost physically sick. She shivered.

Josie looked at her. "Chilly?" She wrapped her arms around herself.

Margaret shook her head. For a few minutes she just sat and worried. Then she got the pen out of her pocket and wrote. "I ought to be going."

For a minute Josie didn't answer. Then she picked up the pad. "If you want to stay and keep an eye on Sonny there, fine with me. Nice to have company. Like it here, but alone too much."

(77)

Margaret felt melted inside with relief. Quickly she wrote, "Love to if no bother."

"No bother. A pleasure." Josie walked around the cabin and climbed into the rope hammock. "Nap time."

Margaret settled back in her chair. She had almost forgotten how great it was to feel free and happy.

9

LATER JOSIE BROUGHT THEIR DINNER UP ON DECK—
wonderful crispy fried conch steaks, black-eyed peas,
and hot buttered johnnycake that was more like baking
powder biscuits than the cornmeal johnnycake Margaret
had known in Maine. There were sliced tomatoes, too,
in some kind of oil dressing. And fresh pineapple for
dessert.

Margaret washed the dishes, and then she and Josie
sat in the bow again and watched the sky turn pink from
the sunset. Boats coming home were dark silhouettes on
pink water against a pink sky. The evening star came
out, hanging in the sky like a jewel.

Margaret wished she knew how to write poetry.
Becky wrote poetry sometimes. She remembered one
about their skating party that night at the pond. It was
called "Night Birds." If she could write poetry, it might
be kind of a substitute for the music she couldn't hear.
Maybe she'd try it sometime. Just for herself.

She looked up as she felt Josie stiffen and sit up straight. A small boat with an outboard motor was coming toward them, with one person in it. It moved slowly, and Margaret could imagine the chug-chug sound it made, like Grandfather's old outboard. She wondered if it were someone Josie knew, because Josie was peering at the boat. She didn't wave, though. Her fishing line was still in the water, and Margaret realized, as the boat came nearer, that if it didn't veer off, it would run right through the line. She wondered why Josie didn't reel it in; maybe the guy in the boat didn't see it.

But Josie just sat waiting. The boat came almost to the line before it suddenly swung out and picked up speed. Close in, Margaret saw it was the woman she had seen on shore. She wanted to ask Josie who it was, but it was too dark to write. The quick glimpse of the woman's face had made Margaret shiver; it looked wild, malevolent.

Sonny was trying to get to his feet, so Margaret went over and helped him up, then loosened the rope a little so he could hobble over to her chair. He kept looking backward, puzzled by the thing that had happened to his hind leg, but he didn't seem to be in pain. Josie went below and brought him up a big head of cabbage. He half leaned against Margaret's chair, munching the cabbage, as if he, too, were happy. She kept her hand on his neck, smoothing down the short, stiff hairs. He was a lovely deer.

After awhile, he turned his head toward the shore, as

if he had heard something. He opened his mouth again, in that little bleating look, and hobbled out to the end of the length of rope. Josie got up and scanned the shore. Finally she pointed to a clump of palms. Almost hidden in the trees and the gathering darkness, a deer was watching them. It was a doe, bigger than Sonny, but still not very big. His mother.

Josie smiled as Margaret stood up and walked over to the rail. They watched the little deer for some time, and Sonny stood alert, his cabbage forgotten. Margaret hoped the doe could see that Sonny was all right.

The fawn turned his head and looked at Margaret with his big, soulful eyes. She wished she could let him talk to his mother, or rub noses or do whatever deer did.

When it got dark, Margaret and Josie went below for a while. Josie made iced tea, and they sat at the table and read, Margaret her *Huck Finn* and Josie a book on horoscopes.

She laughed and pointed to a page under Aries. "You will have a surprise visitor," it said, "but it will be pleasant." Josie touched Margaret's arm. "You." She grinned. "Or Sonny."

At ten o'clock, she washed the iced-tea glasses and said, "Sack time." She got a sleeping bag for Margaret and pointed toward the deck with a question in her raised eyebrows. Margaret nodded. Yes, she wanted to sleep near Sonny.

Margaret spread out the sleeping bag not far from the fawn. She patted his neck and whispered to him before she settled down to sleep. Josie was already tucked into her hammock.

She lay on her back looking up at the black velvety sky with its millions of stars. It looked close enough to pull up to her chin like a comforter. She wondered if the water made that little lapping sound the ocean used to make in Maine when the wind was still. She thought about that sound for a while and then she thought about the rhythmic crash and roar of heavy surf, which she had loved. The water would fly up on the rocks in great lacy curtains of spray. She wondered if this water ever looked like that. They had hurricanes here. There weren't the high rocks, though, for the waves to smash against. That pounding of surf had always reminded her of the Beethoven Fifth, there at the beginning. She listened to it in her mind—da da da *da*.

Once when she had been practicing *Für Elise* by Beethoven, her grandfather had looked over her shoulder at the music and said in his loud, hoarse voice, "Beethoven was deaf, you know." Of course, she knew Beethoven was deaf. Everybody knew that. She'd been practicing for a recital, and she hadn't even bothered to answer her grandfather. Now she wished with all her heart that she could tell him how well she knew what it must have meant to Beethoven to lose his hearing, and what it must have meant to Grandfather. She wondered if you always learned how to understand people after it was too late.

10

WHEN SHE OPENED HER EYES, THE FIRST THING SHE SAW
was Sonny. He was gazing at her steadily, and he flicked
his ears as if to say good morning.

Margaret saw that Josie had already washed down the
bow deck, moving Sonny a little further toward Margaret so she could do a thorough job. Margaret took a
deep breath and smelled coffee. She had slept really hard.
She sat up and reached over to pat Sonny. He lifted his
nose, to show his enjoyment, as she rubbed the tiny
pedicels where his antlers would some day grow. She
hoped he would have very impressive antlers, which
probably bucks longed for the way boys wanted broad
shoulders. She laughed at the idea and got up.

Josie bounded up on deck, bright-eyed and full of
energy. She let down the gangplank, which she had put
up the night before, and called, "Good morning, Skipper." With a shock, Margaret realized that Josie hadn't

even asked her name. Did that mean it really was going to be safe here? She decided it did. And she'd write down *Margaret* for Josie. She owed her that much at least.

After breakfast, Josie took Margaret ashore and helped her get food for Sonny. She pointed out some of the strangely named trees that grew around there: gumbo-limbo, pigeon plum, blolly, buttonwood. Many of them had flowers. She pulled some leaves from a plant called air plant, leaves that would live and grow and send out roots if you just attach them to a window curtain or something. She took a bunch for Sonny to chew on.

When they came onto the boat, their arms full of branches and leaves, Margaret wanted to laugh. We look like the forest of Dunsinane in *Macbeth*, she thought, wondering if Josie had read *Macbeth*. Then she felt one of those sudden spasms of anger that hit her since she'd gotten deaf. What was the good of having something to say if you always had to write it down. Most of it wasn't that important; just the little things that made it fun to be with somebody. By the time you got pen and paper and wrote down a joke, it wasn't funny anymore. And you had to explain: "I was just thinking, when we came on deck, with all these branches . . ." Who cared.

When Josie had gone to work and Sonny was gorging himself on his green breakfast, Margaret decided to go for a swim. She looked at the water off the bow end and decided it was deep enough for a shallow dive. The floor of the Gulf seemed to drop off in a hurry here. She dove off the boat and came up some distance out. Sonny had turned to look at her, when he heard the splash, and now he stood motionless for a moment, with a long palm frond hanging from his mouth. Margaret laughed, feeling a sudden ache of happiness under her ribs. He was such a funny deer, and she loved him so much. What if he had been killed when that stupid pickup hit him . . . but he hadn't been. He was all right, or he would be soon, and he was her little deer. Josie even let her feed him. She'd have to take care of swabbing down the deck, too; Josie shouldn't have to do that.

She swam out in a long, easy crawl stroke, enjoying the cool, smooth water. Looking back, she noticed there was a rope ladder on the port side of the bow. Josie must swim out here, too. It would be nice if they swam together.

Two pelicans hit the water with a splash not far from her. She couldn't tell whether they caught anything or not; their beaks were so big, anything they grabbed would disappear at once. A small heron with a dark blue body skimmed the water and followed the shoreline. It would be nice to be a bird. Well, in some ways. A dangerous life, though. But everybody's life was dangerous. That was something she had discovered with a shock. Somehow the three aunts had managed to make her feel so safe all through her childhood.

She surface dove, staying down as long as she could,

to see what was there. A school of small minnowlike fish went right past her face, and she caught flashes of brightly colored larger fish darting along below her. She saw a starfish that was the color of sunset. They said you could chop a starfish in half and instead of a dead starfish, you'd get two live ones. Never say die, old starfish, she thought—and surfaced, gasping for breath.

Getting tired, finally, she turned on her back and swam slowly toward the boat, lifting her arms in long, lazy strokes. Sonny would be getting lonesome.

She grabbed the rope ladder and held on for a minute, catching her breath. The hull of the boat was encrusted with barnacles. She wondered if Josie had to have it scraped and caulked every year. Probably not, since it wasn't a seagoing boat. She hauled herself up on the rope ladder. -

As her head cleared the deck, she froze. There was a commotion on deck. Sonny was strained back against the bow rail, as far as his rope would let him go, and he was trembling violently. At the stern, standing on the top rung of the gangplank, was the woman Margaret had seen on shore the day before, the one who had almost tangled Josie's fishing line later. She had a big, ugly black dog with her, holding him by the collar. The dog was straining to break loose so he could spring at the fawn.

When the woman saw Margaret, she stepped back in surprise, pointed to Sonny, and began to jabber, her big mouth flapping like a fish out of water. Margaret didn't try for words; she just yelled, putting all the strength she had behind the sound. The woman looked frightened. Dripping wet, Margaret started toward her. The dog almost broke loose from the woman's grasp. Very faintly Margaret could hear the racket of his barking.

She grabbed the first thing she could get her hands on, a folded deck chair. Lifting it over her head, she charged at the dog. The woman turned and ran, stumbling, down the gangplank, hauling the reluctant dog along after her. Margaret stood in the stern, the chair still over her head, letting her voice yell, hoping it was as loud and harsh and threatening as any voice the woman and her mean old dog had ever heard.

When she was sure they were gone, she tried to comfort Sonny. But the dog had frightened him badly, and it was a long time before he stopped shaking and cowering against the bow rail. From then until Josie came home, Margaret sat beside him, trying to calm him, trying to calm herself.

11

JOSIE CAME UP THE GANGPLANK PUSHING HER BIKE, looking excited and happy. She was balancing a long box on the bicycle, and she called out something.

Margaret didn't understand so she went closer, and Josie repeated it.

"Got a present. Danny. Birthday present."

Josie looked so happy that for a moment Margaret forgot her anxiety.

Josie stood the bike near the cabin and took the package off. It was big. "From Russia." Her eyes shone, and she hefted the box carefully.

Margaret went below and got the machete so Josie could cut the many strings. Hunched down on the deck beside Josie, she watched the slow, methodical unwrapping. What, she wondered, would someone in the Merchant Marine send his mother from Russia? She wished she had known it was Josie's birthday. It would have been fun to get her a present.

As if she had read Margaret's mind, Josie said, "He's always early."

Margaret formed the word "when."

"Tuesday." She pulled off an outer layer of wrapping paper, broke a seal, and started on the next one, talking away happily. More strings came off and more paper, until she got down to a box. She paused and looked at it and looked up at Margaret. "Guess."

Margaret studied it, then made the motions of playing a violin.

Josie laughed. "Maybe." She touched the box lightly. "Small bowling alley?"

Margaret pointed to some words on the box, written in Cyrillic script. Josie slit open the end of the box and felt inside. She pulled out a handful of torn paper padding. She pulled out more torn-up paper until it was heaped on the deck. "Something in here . . ." Slowly she pulled.

Margaret moved so she could see better. It *was* some kind of musical instrument. Not a violin, though. Josie was talking, but she had her head down so Margaret didn't know what she was saying. She pulled out the neck of a stringed instrument. A long, narrow neck, with frets. She kept pulling, very carefully, until suddenly the whole thing came free of the box.

Josie held it up. It was a fragile-looking, graceful instrument; the sound box was small, with curved sides. Josie looked up at her. "What is it?"

Margaret knew what it was, but she couldn't think of

the name. She stood up, teetering on her toes in an effort to get the name. It was right on the end of her tongue. It was a Russian instrument and what was it called? A balalaika! That was it. She reached for the little pencil in Josie's pocket and wrote "Balalaika" on a piece of the wrapping paper.

Josie tried the word slowly. "Bal-a-lai-ka?"

Margaret wrote it phonetically, with the accent mark, "Bal-a-líke-a." Then she added, "Russian folk music." Josie took it down to the bow, absently patting Sonny as she went past him. Sonny jerked his head back and trembled, and she gave him a quick glance. "What is it?" she said to Margaret.

Margaret didn't want to tell her about the woman just now and spoil her pleasure, so she said nothing. Josie sat down in her favorite chair, put her feet up on the railing, and began to tune the instrument.

Margaret found herself straining to hear the sounds as Josie plucked the strings. In her mind she tried to imagine them, although she had never heard a balalaika. Would it be like a guitar? Probably a more fragile sound. Oh, if she could only hear—

Josie caught the look of pain on Margaret's face. She stopped fiddling with the strings for a moment. "You like music?" She repeated it. "Like music?"

Margaret nodded. She tried to smile.

Josie's dark eyes were sympathetic. "Used to play?" She held the balalaika as if she were playing a violin.

Margaret held out her hands to indicate a piano key-board.

Josie didn't speak for a minute. "How long have you been deaf? How long?" She touched Margaret's ear.

Margaret held up one finger, and indicated the tip of another one.

Josie shook her head and looked away, frowning, staring out at the sea.

Margaret was sorry she had made Josie feel sad, just when she had been so happy. She touched Josie's arm, and pointed to the balalaika, strumming the air with her fingers.

Josie gave her a quick, bright smile. "All right." She bent her head over the instrument and tried a few chords, then looked up and nodded. "Nice."

For quite a while Margaret sat on the deck with her back against the railing, watching Josie coax tunes out of the balalaika, trying to read the music from the movement of Josie's fingers. At last she gave up; it made her head ache, trying to hear with her mind. She got up and swept up the debris from the package. Sonny hobbled toward her as far as his rope would let him go. When she put the broom away, she sat down on the deck beside him, and he nuzzled close to her, rubbing his black nose against her shoulder.

Josie came over and examined his leg. "He's nervous." She looked at Margaret. "Anything happen?"

Margaret hesitated. But when Josie asked a question,

you just about had to answer it. She wrote it down, about the woman and the black dog.

Josie frowned. After a minute she wrote quickly. "The Carter woman." She touched her finger to her head, and then wrote, "Ignorant. Harmless. But that dog isn't." She tapped the pencil against her teeth. "Let's go see her."

Margaret went below and changed quickly from her bathing suit to her jeans and shirt. The money Ed had given her was still safe in her pocket. She wondered what to do with it. She glanced around the cabin quickly, and then smoothed out the bills and put them under the pillow on the top bunk.

When they were both ashore, Josie shoved the gangplank in place with a pole. She had to wade into the water to secure the chain, but she paid no attention to the fact that her sneakers were soaking wet. She also caught the end of the rope ladder and threw it up onto the deck, so no one could use it to get aboard. Margaret wondered how they were going to get back on the boat themselves, but she was sure it would be no problem to Josie.

They went single file along the same path they had come yesterday morning. It seemed weeks ago, not just yesterday. Key West seemed a million miles away. She thought about her mother, wondering if she and Ed were married yet. How long did it take to get a marriage license? And where would they go on their honeymoon? Ed went to the Bahamas and places like that quite a lot. Her mother would have a nice life, and no problem child to spoil it.

Josie branched off onto another path, even fainter than the first one. In a minute she pointed to an empty cabin set back in a grove of palmettos. It was a neat little cabin, silvered by the weather. Josie got a key from a hook over the door and unlocked the padlock. It was dark and cool inside, empty of furniture except for an old rocker and a couch. There were two small rooms and a kitchen alcove.

Josie checked the window. She rattled the knob of one of the wooden shutters to make sure it was firmly in place. Then she locked the padlock again, and they came out into the light. "My cabin," Josie said. "Good for strong weather."

In a few minutes they came to another, larger cabin. The front door and the jalousies on the front were open, and there was wash hanging on a line strung from one palm tree to another. The Carter woman appeared in the doorway and shaded her eyes, watching them approach. Margaret hung back a little, as Josie marched up the path. Even though Josie had said "harmless," the woman's wild look scared her.

She did not, of course, know what they were saying, but the set of Josie's narrow shoulders looked stern, and the woman was obviously shouting. Several times she glared past Josie at Margaret. There was no sign of the dog.

Margaret tensed as the woman took a threatening step

(*94*)

toward Josie, but Josie didn't give an inch. She lifted her arm and wagged her finger at the woman, and then she turned away and came back toward Margaret. As they walked down the path, Margaret looked back. The woman, still standing on her doorsill, shook her fist.

Josie looked calm. "Trashy people," she said.

Margaret shivered and restrained the impulse to look over her shoulder again. Once she wouldn't have given a second thought to a woman like that, but just because she couldn't hear her, the woman scared her.

12

JOSIE WORKED SEVEN DAYS A WEEK, SO THE WEEKENDS were no different from other days. Margaret fell into a pleasant routine of her own: swimming, reading, sunbathing, cleaning up the boat, exploring the shore at low tide, and taking care of Sonny.

He learned to balance himself better after a few days. Margaret walked him up and down the deck several times a day, leading him on the rope. He was nervous at first, but then he grew to like the walks, and when she reached for his rope, his big ears would twitch and he would push her with his black nose. Sometimes he almost lost his balance, but she was there to help him.

Whenever she sat down near him, he liked to put his head in her lap, and sometimes he tried to climb into her lap like a dog. He was too long to fit, and his injured leg got in the way, but he got as close to her as he could. It reminded her of the one dog she had ever had, a beagle

pup that Aunt Ethel had brought home for her. Her mother didn't like dogs, and she kept looking for an excuse to get rid of him. Finally, when he chewed up one of her best shoes, she made such a fuss that Aunt Ethel took him back to the farm where she had bought him. Both Margaret and Aunt Ethel had cried.

Probably when Sonny was all well, she would have to leave. Josie had said "stay and look after Sonny." Each day that went by made the thought of leaving more painful. It would be a long, lonely trip to Maine.

She had read most of Josie's books. There were three Agatha Christies and two Patricia Highsmiths, a book by Pearl Buck that she hadn't started yet, a beautiful little copy of *The Rubaiyat of Omar Khayyam* bound in soft red leather, with an inscription inside that said, "Merry Christmas, Mom. Love, *Danny*." Margaret had read most of it, and some of it she liked to read aloud to Sonny. "Listen, Sonny," she'd say to him, "this is pretty."

> Whether we wake or we sleep,
> Whether we carol or weep,
> The sun with his Planets in chime,
> Marketh the going of Time.

And Sonny would gaze at her with his big, dark eyes.

But best of all she loved the little book called *Seashores*. It had pictures and descriptions of shells and sea plants and shore birds. She also studied the well-worn book on birds that Josie was always getting out to identify some bird or other. The birds were interesting, but it was the marine life that most fascinated Margaret. At home she had never paid particular attention to sea life, but here there was such an abundance and it was so odd and interesting, she could hardly wait for low tide every day to see what she could find.

Josie went with her when she was there. She was always looking for shells to use in her necklaces and things, but she helped Margaret find and identify specimens, too. She brought home some plastic buckets and some flat oblong plastic trays. Together they found and gathered different kinds of marine algae and put them in a bucket of salt water. Later, on the boat, Margaret carefully separated them, the way the little book said, floating one plant at a time in one of the oblong containers. Then she slipped a piece of paper under the plant, lifted it out of the tray, and covered it with cheesecloth. Finally she blotted it dry, mounted it on another piece of paper, and labeled it. It took a lot of patience, but she really enjoyed it.

She had always had a good memory for anything that interested her, and she amazed Josie with how quickly she learned. Concentrating on something like that helped keep her mind off the future. She was, of course, no closer to solving that problem than she'd ever been. But it was hard to think about.

It was fun, studying and classifying, but the best fun

was wading in the warm, shallow water at low tide, trying to find the plants and animals.

Once Margaret took Sonny down to the shore with her, helping him down the gangplank, and keeping the rope handy, although it was unlikely he would try to wander off. He stepped on a couple of shells and a plant that she wanted, but most of the time he chewed contentedly on the shrubs that lined the shore. There was no real beach near Josie's boat, just a thin stretch of muddy sand at low tide. And there were lots of basins that tide and weather had worn in the soft limestone of the Key. These were wonderful places to find things. One afternoon Margaret lay on her stomach on the damp ground for a long time, staring into a pool at a kelp crab.

On the day before her birthday, Josie came home from work with a stack of comic books that someone had left in a room. She and Margaret sat on the deck reading and swapping "Mandrake the Magician," "The Green Hornet," "Prince Valiant," even a few "Donald Duck" adventures. Margaret hadn't looked at a comic book for years, but it was fun. Josie laughed with delight at all of them. She told Margaret that she and Danny had read comics together when he was a boy.

Margaret felt a pang of envy. What fun it would be to have a mother who read the comics with you. She wished she could stay with Josie forever. But naturally, Josie wouldn't want that. She didn't even know Margaret, really. It was odd to think how short a time they had known each other; Margaret felt as if she'd known

Josie all her life. The next day, in the morning, after Josie went to work, Margaret had decided she was going to look for a store. There had to be a store somewhere, because Josie brought home groceries, magazines, and things. Margaret was going to buy Josie a birthday present, though she had no idea what it was going to be. And she was going to make a cake.

13

ALMOST AS SOON AS JOSIE HAD LEFT FOR WORK, MARGARET got ready for her shopping trip. She combed her hair carefully and put on a clean shirt. She got the money from under the pillow on the bunk and put it in her shirt pocket, neatly folded.

She told Sonny where she was going. "Just be good while I'm gone. It won't be long. Don't get nervous and don't step on the starfish." She checked his rope to make sure it was fastened securely. "I'll bring you a present, too."

Sonny munched thoughtfully on a palm frond and looked at her. She gave him a hug. "I don't think anybody will bother you. Josie put the fear of God into that woman with the dog."

Just to be safe, she not only hauled up the gangplank but also tossed the rope ladder over the rail, as Josie had done. She could scramble up the pine tree on the starboard side and drop down onto the deck, the way Josie had.

She walked quickly down the path. It felt funny to be going somewhere. Her little world at the boat had so completely engrossed her, she had hardly thought of a world beyond it. In fact, she had tried to forget. She hoped she could find a store.

When she got to the highway, she turned left, because she knew from what Josie had said that the motel where she worked was toward the right, toward Key West.

She passed a big luxury motel that had a sign about seeing the dolphins. She'd like to see some dolphins. But first she had to find the store. She walked along the edge of the road. The usual mild breeze had sharpened to a real wind, and every now and then the sun was obscured by scudding clouds. She wondered if that meant rain in this country.

She hadn't even wished Josie a happy birthday! She wanted her to think she hadn't remembered it, so she would be all the more surprised when she got home.

Ahead of her she saw a little cluster of stores: a gas station and restaurant, a bar, a grocery store, and a shop that advertised GIFTS—CURIOS. She braced herself and went into the grocery store. Shopping was difficult when you couldn't hear. The man at the cash register was busy talking to another man, and he only glanced and nodded at Margaret.

She looked among the jumbled shelves, hunting for the cake mixes. She found them finally, and picked out a devil's-food mix. Josie liked chocolate. Next to the cake mixes she found a box of white frosting mix. Then Margaret hunted for birthday candles, trying to think where whoever had stocked this untidy store would think of putting birthday candles. She couldn't find them. It was taking her a long time and she was getting more and more jumpy. She glanced quickly toward the front of the store. The other man had gone, and the proprietor was watching her. She thought of the sign the man at home had put up in the window of his little grocery store: DUE TO SHOPLIFTING, NO MORE THAN TWO PEOPLE UNDER THE AGE OF 18 ALLOWED IN THIS STORE AT A TIME UNLESS SUPERVIZED BY PARENTS. When the sign first went up, Becky had gone in and told him he'd misspelled *supervised*. He got very mad and chased her out. If you were a teenager, Margaret thought, you must be some kind of criminal. And if you were a stone-deaf teenager, you were really a dangerous character. She'd almost forgotten that on the houseboat.

She gave up on the candles, remembered powdered sugar, and took her packages to the counter. She didn't look at the man. If she did, he might say something, and she was too nervous to try to lip-read a stranger. She watched the cash register instead, then fumbled in her pocket for her money. She had folded the bills so carefully she had to unfold all four of them to take one out. The man stood looking at her, probably thinking she had stolen the money. She wanted to yell at him: "How could I shoplift when you can see all I've got is these little tiny pockets?" But she just handed him a twenty-dollar bill. He took forever counting out the change. When she had it at last, she grabbed her bag of groceries and fled, shaken and angry.

Margaret wished she could go right straight back to the boat, but she hadn't gotten the present yet. For a long time she stood outside the gift shop, peering at things in the window and trying to see what was inside. Lots of shells. Monkey faces made out of coconut shells. Millions of postcards. Jars of Key lime marmalade. Cameras and film. She thought for a moment about getting a camera. But Josie might have one.

Well, she'd never find anything standing outside. She took a deep breath and went in. A plump middle-aged woman sat at the counter doing a crossword puzzle. She looked up, smiled, and said something. It looked like "Good morning." Margaret nodded and went down to the back of the shop. Souvenir ashtrays; more shells; little bottles of perfume. Perfume? No, Josie wasn't the type, and it was probably cheap perfume anyway. She was so intent on finding something, she forgot for a moment to be nervous. But suddenly she realized the woman was standing next to her, talking to her. Margaret attempted a smile and moved away. She was shivering although it was warm in the shop. She looked at some little glass birds and fish, and for a second she considered them. But they weren't good enough for Josie. It had to be something really special.

The woman hovered near her. She had stopped smiling. Fortunately, someone came in, a woman who looked like a tourist. Margaret could see the woman's husband, or whoever it was, waiting outside with that blank, patient look men seem to get when they have to wait for their wives to shop. The saleslady had to leave Margaret and wait on the woman, but she kept glancing back.

Then Margaret saw a pair of binoculars, and she knew instantly that that was for Josie. She could imagine Josie leaning over the bow rail, training the glasses on some bird. Margaret picked them up and looked through them. Oh, Josie would like these!

She took them to the counter, waiting impatiently while the saleslady hovered over the new customer. The saleslady kept glancing at Margaret and at the binoculars. Finally, she came over to the counter and said something. Margaret got the word "help." She must have said, "Can I help you?" Margaret held out the binoculars. The woman looked at her sharply and said something else.

Margaret remembered she hadn't read the price tag. She reached out and turned it around so she could see it. Forty-two dollars. That was a bit startling; she hadn't realized they would cost that much. But it was all right; it was for Josie. She pulled the money out of her pocket and gave the woman the forty-two dollars. It gave her real satisfaction to see the woman's look of surprise. However, the woman said something else. Margaret shook her head. The woman raised her voice. Margaret looked at the cash register. Tax. She owed the sales tax. She gave the woman the money.

The woman's attitude changed at once. She even smiled as she put the binoculars in a box and gift wrapped them. Margaret thought of something her grandfather used to say: "Money makes the mare go."

When she got outside the shop, Margaret felt so happy she wanted to shout and dance. She had never dreamed she'd find anything so right for Josie. Now Josie wouldn't have to wonder whether the bird off the bow was a sooty tern or a bridled tern. She'd be able to tell! Margaret hugged the box under her arm, almost wishing the woman hadn't wrapped it, so she could take the glasses out again and look at them. But the box did look pretty.

On the way home, she detoured around to the back of the big motor hotel that advertised the dolphins. She couldn't stay long because she had to bake the cake before Josie got home, but she did want to see the dolphins.

They were in an enormous salt water pool that was separated from the Gulf by a seawall. There were pretty gardens on the far side of the pool, and tables and chairs. A sign said there was a telephone under the next palm tree, where you could phone to the bar for drinks. Margaret leaned over the rail of the bridge, which stretched over the pool, for several minutes before she saw the dolphin. As far as she could see, there was only one, but he was worth stopping to see. He had a little white rubber raft, the kind people play with in swimming pools. He kept coming up under it so that it was on his head. Then he'd swim like mad all around the pool, wearing this rakish little hat. It would fall off, and he'd dive again and come up under it. Sometimes he pushed it with his nose, very fast. Once he surfaced just below Margaret and looked up at her with his dark, intelligent eyes. He almost seemed about to speak to her.

"Hi," she said. There was no one around so she risked saying it aloud. "You are beautiful."

He looked at her steadily for a long moment, his gray head wet and sleek. She wished she could reach him, touch that smooth head. The dolphin made a sudden turn and a spectacular leap out of the water. Margaret caught the flash of his white underside and the yellow bands along his flanks. He dove, leaped again, and swam around the big pool with incredible speed.

Finally tearing herself away, she thought that there was a creature she'd like to have for a friend. If you had a Key deer of your very own, your own dolphin, and a whole bunch of sea creatures, you wouldn't need people. Except Josie. She'd always want Josie around. But Josie might not always want her. She put the disturbing thought into the back of her mind and walked fast toward home.

14

EVERYTHING WAS READY. THE CAKE, BAKED AND FROSTED, sat in the center of the table. The frosting had run a little but otherwise it looked fine. Margaret stuck three of Josie's long wooden matches into the cake, and when Josie came, she would light them. They wouldn't burn long, but they would have to do as candles.

The binoculars were on the bunk in Margaret's cabin, to be brought out after dinner. She had cut off an end of the ribbon and made a bow for Sonny, tied into the rope he wore around his neck. It was a vivid blue bow, and it made him look very handsome, though he kept trying to eat it.

In a fruit juice bottle Margaret arranged a big bouquet of pink oleanders that she had picked on the way home. She had intended to give some of the big glossy leaves to Sonny for the present she had promised him, but fortunately she had made it a habit to check Josie's books before she gave him anything new. She discovered that the juice of the oleander is poisonous. So she went ashore again and got him some more of the thatch palm that he loved.

Just for fun she laid out a hand of solitaire on the table, all ready for Josie. Josie liked to play, and she had been teaching Margaret gin rummy. Margaret was intrigued with the cards; they were a very old deck that said "Intercolonial Railway and Prince Edward Island Railway of Canada," and each card had a scene in the middle, "Falls at Little Métis, Lower St. Lawrence," "Salmon Fishing, Matapedia River," and so on. They had belonged to Josie's father, and she didn't know where he had gotten them. He had probably taken a trip up there when he was a young man, she said. Margaret wrote down on the pad of paper that her home was not far from Prince Edward Island. Josie had looked interested, but she hadn't asked for more information. She never did. It made Margaret want to tell her more. But so far she hadn't. It was too much to write. And besides, she didn't know just how much to say, without saying too much.

Several times Margaret had almost begun to talk to Josie. She wanted to terribly; it would make communication so much easier, and there were lots of things she could say, wanted to say. But when she got ready to speak, she lost her nerve. It seemed as if the silence she had wrapped herself in for so long, had become a kind of armor that she couldn't break out of. She spent more time talking to Sonny, trying to get used to speaking aloud. But it wasn't being used to it that mattered; it was the idea of talking out loud to another human being. Sonny didn't care how she sounded.

She went up on deck and took Sonny some fresh water. "Don't get your bow wet," she told him. "You look gorgeous. Remember to sing 'Happy Birthday' when Josie comes." She laughed at the look he gave her. "Sometimes I think you understand English." She fluffed up the bow. The wind was making the boat rock a little. The water, usually so calm, was stirred up in small waves. "Light chop," as the weather notice in the paper had predicted.

She looked out at the thin strip of land that ran out into the Gulf, a little farther along the shore. It had low, brushy vegetation, and it was no more than a dozen feet wide. That morning after she woke up, she thought she saw two deer over there, but she hadn't been sure. Josie had looked, too, and she'd said, "Probably. Hard to tell from here." But with the binoculars, they'd be able to tell. Margaret wondered if Sonny's mother still came back at night to check up on him. She had not seen her again. Josie said deer stayed in pretty much the same territory all the time, as long as there was food.

When it was time for Josie to come, Margaret stationed herself at the gangplank, watching. She was impatient, eager for Josie to see her cake. She hoped she'd be pleased. Maybe she would rather have had white cake with chocolate frosting. Or angel food cake? Well, no time to think of that now. She looked at her Timex watch. Josie was late. She had probably gone to buy groceries. Margaret worried about that, about eating up Josie's groceries. She tried to think how she could give Josie some of her money to buy food with, without insulting her. Maybe she would just have to go to that grocery store again by herself and bring some things home. That might be more tactful than offering Josie money. Josie was awfully independent about things . . .

She straightened up. Josie was coming! She could just see the top of the straw hat, bobbing along through the foliage. It was a temptation to race down the gangplank and greet her, but she made herself wait.

Josie came into sight, wheeling the bike. The wire basket that held her broom and buckets also had bags of groceries. As she came up the gangplank, she said, "Hi. Busy day. People dirtier than ever." She looked tired.

Margaret took the bike from her, wheeled it up the ramp, and unloaded the groceries. Holding up her hands to tell Josie to wait before she went below, Margaret hurried down with the groceries and put them on the floor; she'd unpack them later. She checked everything quickly. If only the frosting hadn't run. Tremulous with excitement, she raced up the iron steps. Josie, patting Sonny, looked up, smiling and curious.

"He looks beautiful." She pointed to Sonny's bow.

Margaret took her hand and led her to the cabin. They had to brace themselves a little against the gentle pitch of the boat. Margaret went down ahead of Josie, and at the bottom of the steps took Josie's hands and put them over her eyes.

Smiling and obedient, Josie stood with her hands over her eyes. Margaret struck a match and lit the three matches that were stuck into the cake. Then she pulled Josie's hands away from her eyes and stood aside.

For a long minute Josie stood perfectly still, looking at the cake with its flaring matches, at the flowers, at the deck of cards neatly laid out. She looked so long that Margaret began to panic. She doesn't like it, she thought; it's too gaudy; she maybe hates surprises . . . But then Josie looked at her, and her dark eyes shone with such emotion, Margaret had to look away, afraid she herself was going to cry. She grabbed the pad of paper and wrote "Happy Birthday, dear Josie, happy birthday to you . . ." and she grabbed the wooden spoon that she had mixed the cake with. Mouthing the words of the Happy Birthday song, she beat out the rhythm of it on the edge of the table.

Josie threw her head back and laughed. She put her hands on Margaret's waist and danced her around and around the table, both of them laughing till the tears rolled down their cheeks.

Josie collapsed into a chair. She gazed at the cake admiringly. "You went to the store?" When Margaret nodded, she looked at her thoughtfully. "That took nerve, didn't it?"

Margaret shrugged. No use to carry on about how

much nerve it did take. Josie was happy, so it was all worthwhile.

"And the oleanders . . ." She touched a petal. Then she said, "You didn't give Sonny . . ."

Margaret shook her head and pointed to the book on flowers.

"Good girl." She started unpacking the groceries. "Turtle steaks. Okay?"

Margaret clutched her stomach and rolled her eyes in ecstasy. She adored turtle steaks, as Josie already knew.

Josie laughed. She took out one of the huge alligator pears that were the Keys' equivalent of the avocados Margaret had occasionally had at home. There was also a box of guava shells and a package of cream cheese, for a Cuban dessert Josie had tried to describe. And some plantains. Now Margaret would find out what you did with them. Finally, there was something Margaret didn't recognize at all; it looked a little like sweet potatoes but not really. She pointed to it.

"Malanga," Josie said. She wrote the word down. "Very good." She put the milk, the eggs, and the sack of oranges away in the refrigerator. "Swim?" she said.

Margaret nodded eagerly. A swim was just what she needed to cool herself off. It wasn't hot, really not nearly as hot as it had been, but the excitement made her skin feel as if it were burning.

She got into her suit and joined Josie on deck. Josie dived off first, a nice clean dive right through an incoming wave. Josie was a neat swimmer. Margaret looked up

at a gull that was circling over her head, mentally said "hi, gull," and dove in. The water was about the same temperature as the air. She stroked hard to catch up with Josie, and then they swam side by side for some distance, farther than usual, before Josie finally turned around and started back. She swam without a cap, and her dark hair was plastered to her head. Her eyes sparkled. She yelled something and headed for shore.

Margaret guessed that she said, "Beat you to the boat," and she swam as fast as she could, but Josie beat her. Josie always beat. She swam like a fish.

The wind was too cool for lying on deck in wet bathing suits. They dressed and put on sweaters. Josie curled up in her hammock for a nap, and Margaret settled down with the seashore book. After a good wind like this one, a lot of interesting things would be washed up on the shore.

But she was feeling too pleased with life to concentrate. She kept remembering how happy Josie had looked about the cake. Wait till she saw the binoculars!

The boat rocked, the keel grating a little on the sand. She could feel the little tremor the grating made. She sat closer to Sonny, and took off his ribbon, which seemed to bother him. He was nervous about the wind. With each movement of the boat, he braced his feet as if he expected to fall, and his eyes looked wide and frightened. Margaret petted him and talked to him.

"It's just wind. It won't hurt you. It won't be a hurricane or anything. When there's a big wind, Josie moves back to her cabin. And here we are, right here, Sonny, so this isn't going to be a big wind. Anyway, we'd take care of you, first thing."

Her voice seemed to soothe him, and after a while he stopped trembling and jerking, but he wouldn't lie down. She untied him and walked him to the other end of the boat, keeping her arm around him so the motion of the boat wouldn't throw him off balance. She leaned against the rail, watching the trees swaying in the wind. She wished she could hear it; she'd always liked the sound of wind.

She noticed a pair of bright eyes looking at them from the shelter of a scrub palmetto. It was the raccoon she had seen several times before. He was much paler than the raccoons at home, and you could hardly see the rings on his tail. Josie said he was called the Big Pine raccoon.

"Hi, Raccoon," Margaret said. "It's Josie's birthday."

The raccoon stood up on his hind legs to get a better look at them. Margaret liked him because he was so bright-eyed and so fearless.

"I'll tell her you said happy birthday," she said. As she walked Sonny back along the deck, she thought, It's a good thing I can't talk to people; the things I think of to say are so kooky, they'd lock me up.

She tied Sonny's rope to the rail and lay down near him on her stomach, watching the moving sea that was the color of pewter now. Josie's hammock swayed gently in the wind. It was a very good day.

15

THE DINNER WAS ESPECIALLY GOOD. THE TURTLE STEAKS were cooked to perfection; the malanga, peeled and boiled and doused in melted butter with garlic; the plantain, cut very thin and fried like French fried potatoes; the avocados, sprinkled with Josie's good oil and vinegar dressing; and for dessert there was not only the birthday cake, but also the guava shells with cream cheese. Margaret thought she had never tasted anything so good as those guava shells, preserved in syrup.

They took a long time eating, and Margaret joined Josie in a cup of Cuban coffee so strong it made her gasp. Josie drank half a cup several times a day. Margaret liked to watch her make it. She put the coffee in a flannel bag, put the bag on a little iron tripod down in an enamel pot, and poured boiling water over it. The water filtered through the coffee and into the bottom of the pot. It was an unusual way to make coffee. But then it was unusual coffee, at least to Margaret. Sometimes at home Aunt Tillie had given her some coffee, but it had always had lots of milk in it and it was about as strong as water. She wished she could tell Josie about the aunts.

It was time to get the present. For a minute Margaret put it off, feeling suddenly shy. But while Josie stacked the dishes in the sink, Margaret got up her nerve and went into her cabin. Josie's back was toward her. She put the box on the table in Josie's place and waited.

When Josie turned around and saw it, she looked even more astonished than she had when she saw the cake. She just stared at the box and stared at Margaret and stared at the box again. "For me?" she said finally.

Margaret nodded, grinning. She couldn't wait for Josie to open it.

Josie took forever, folding the ribbon, folding the paper, and then just looking at the unwrapped box. Margaret was beside herself with impatience. She reached out and gave the box a little push toward Josie.

Slowly Josie took off the cover, pulled aside the tissue paper, and looked into the box. She looked up at Margaret with a puzzled frown.

She doesn't like it, Margaret thought. She already has some. She doesn't want them. She clasped her hands together in anguish.

Josie lifted the binoculars out of the box as if they were fragile glass. She lifted them up and looked through them all around the cabin. She lowered them and touched the soft leather strap and examined the lenses.

When at last she looked at Margaret, there were tears in her eyes. "They're beautiful," she said.

Margaret sighed in relief. Josie did like them.

"I always wanted some." She grabbed the pad of paper that was always handy. "For birds especially. But, Skipper, they're so . . ." Josie paused and shook her head. ". . . expensive. You shouldn't have."

Margaret wished she could say something, like: if you want a different size or color, I've got the sales slip. Just some dumb little joke, so Josie would know she hadn't just found them or stolen them or anything. But it was too hard to write that kind of thing down. A remark like that depended on your tone of voice.

Josie still looked bemused. She stared through the glasses at Margaret. Then her face broke into a happy grin. She reached out and squeezed Margaret's hand. "Thank you, Skipper. I'll never forget this."

Margaret went into Josie's cabin and got the balalaika. She put it in Josie's hands and strummed the air with her fingers. Even if she couldn't hear it, she thought it would be appropriate to have music.

Josie tuned the balalaika, bending her head over the strings. Then she leaned back in the chair and began to play. Margaret watched her hands intently. From the motion she could get a sense of the beat. It almost seemed as if, in a minute, she would hear the music, if she just tried hard enough.

Too full of happiness to sit still, she got up and did a little dance around the table. But she knew she probably wasn't matching the steps to the music. She made a little face of frustration and stopped.

"Keep on." Josie nodded encouragingly at her.

Margaret shrugged and shook her head.

"Try it. Watch the beat." Josie brought her hand down on the strings, exaggerating the beat, and stood up to give Margaret more room. "Listen to the music." She tapped her chest. "Inside."

Margaret tried again. She forgot to be self-conscious. Catching the rhythm of Josie's playing, she danced around the table faster and faster until she finally fell into the chair, laughing and breathless. It had been fun.

Josie stopped playing abruptly and cocked her head up, listening. Something was happening above. Margaret didn't even pause to find out what Josie had heard. All she could think of was Sonny. She raced up the steps to the deck. It was dark, and it had started to rain. The wind was blowing. Through the darkness she could see that something was wrong with Sonny. The outline of his body was twisted, somehow. Without even realizing that she was speaking, she called back, "Josie! Come quick. It's Sonny." She ran along the deck to him, almost falling at a sudden pitch of the boat.

When she reached him, she saw at once what had happened. He'd gotten himself tangled up in the rope, and it was choking him. He was trying to stand on his one good hind leg, his front feet in the air, to take the pressure off his neck, but he kept losing his balance. Margaret scooped him up in her arms and held him with all his feet off the deck, to relieve the strain on his neck. He was breathing hard, and his eyes were wild with fear.

In seconds Josie was beside them, untying the rope. Margaret sank down on the wet deck, holding Sonny close, crooning in his ear. Josie disappeared and came back in a few minutes with some blankets, a cloth, and a kettle of hot water. She soaked the cloth in the water and gently washed him all over. That done, she lowered a canvas flap that was part of the awning, and attached it to the rail, to keep off the worst of the rain. And then she put one blanket on the deck and wrapped the other one around Sonny. The three of them sat there for a long time, until Sonny stopped shaking.

Margaret knew now that she had to talk to Josie. There were too many things to be said. Trying to keep her voice steady, she said, "I'll stay with him. He's scared of the wind. He might choke himself again." She spoke slowly, hoping the words were clear, remembering what she'd read about deaf people having a tendency to drop the *s*'s, *t*'s, and *d*'s. Breathe right, she told herself. Open your throat.

Josie made no reply, and Margaret was afraid she hadn't made herself understood, but in a few minutes she went away again, and when she came back, she had warm coats, a thermos of coffee, and a flashlight. She brought Margaret's sleeping bag, and then she brought another one. She sat down beside Margaret and turned the light on her own face so Margaret could read her lips. "He'll be all right. We'll sit up with him."

(*122*)

"You ought to sleep," Margaret said. "You have to go to work."

The light flashed on again. Josie pointed to herself. "Tough cookie." She poured some coffee into the top of the thermos and offered it to Margaret. It was hot and strong and good.

After a while Margaret began to talk. She told Josie about Maine, about the aunts, about her grandfather and the house where they all lived. She talked about skating parties and lobstering and playing in piano recitals. She talked about Becky, Michael, Peter, Linda, and Miss Snow. She didn't talk about her illness, and she didn't mention her mother. She didn't say how she happened to be in Florida, but the talking was like a great load of ice melting inside her—

It was such a relief that when she finished, she leaned back on the sleeping bag and fell asleep exhausted.

16

MARGARET SLEPT LATE IN THE MORNING. WHEN SHE finally sat up and looked around, Sonny was watching her, with his usual absorbed gaze, but Josie wasn't in sight.

The sun was out, and the wind had died down to a gentle breeze, although the sea was still choppy. Margaret yawned, got up and folded the blanket that had been over her, and went below.

There was a note from Josie thumbtacked to the table. "Had a couple errands, left early. See you later. Eat a good breakfast. Love, *J*."

It was lonesome without her. She picked up a newspaper clipping that Josie had left on the table beside the note. BULL RIDER SAYS DEAFNESS HELPS was the headline. It was about a young rodeo champion who had been deaf from birth. He had made two all-around championships, the news item said, and he had a roomful of

(*124*)

trophies. Margaret sat down to finish reading it. He said he couldn't hear the buzzer that signaled the end of the eight-second ride, but he had gotten so he could judge how long eight seconds were. "My deafness has been an asset because I've had to develop great powers of concentration," he said. Josie had penciled in a phrase in the margin: "The law of compensation."

"Well," Margaret said aloud, "I can always become a rodeo rider if things get tough." The clipping and the note depressed her. It meant Josie was encouraging her to do something about her deafness, find some way to overcome the handicap. But she didn't know how, and she didn't want to think about it. For the first time since she'd lost her hearing, she was happy. Why spoil it? Why drum up a lot of new problems, just to show she could cope? She didn't want to do anything but stay with Josie and Sonny. Yet she knew that wasn't realistic. But what could she do?

She sighed and got up to fix some breakfast.

When she had fed herself and Sonny, she wandered around the boat restlessly. She was anxious to see what the storm had washed ashore, but it would be best to do that at low tide. So she decided to go for a walk. Josie had said there was a pond not far away that had an alligator in it. She checked on Sonny's rope. He seemed quiet and happy, chewing away on his breakfast.

She pulled the gangplank up after her and tossed the rope ladder over the side. It was cooler than it had been, and the air was filled with the smell of flowers and recent rain. She walked slowly, stopping to look at different plants and trees. And she kept a sharp lookout for snakes. Josie had told her to be careful, and she had shown her pictures of the different poisonous snakes. It made Margaret a little nervous. Later, when she could afford it, if she were still here, she'd get some boots that came up high. Josie had a pair of real snake boots that Danny had bought her. They cost around a hundred dollars, and were really rugged.

She turned off on a path that angled away into dense vegetation, thinking about the birthday party and about how nice it had been to talk to Josie. She would get Josie to tell her whenever her voice rose too loud or got so soft no one could hear her. Maybe, with Josie to coach her, she could learn to tell by the feeling in her diaphragm just how loud she was talking. It would be a great relief to be able to speak to people, even if she couldn't hear them.

She came to the pond. It was larger than she had expected, with a white sandy beach and a lot of vegetation: small pines, scrub palmetto, and thick brush. Some kind of coarse grass grew out into the pond. A big log lay alongside the grass. Three of the biggest ducks she had ever seen paddled in the shallow water. If she'd known they were there, she would have brought some bread for them.

She walked slowly around the pond, looking for the alligator, but she couldn't see him. Maybe he was underwater. She had never seen a live alligator. When she had walked all around the pond, she sat down on the sand to wait. He'd have to come up some time.

The sun made her warm. The pond, which was down in a little hollow, was protected from the breeze, and she half dozed on the coarse white sand.

Her mind was vaguely planning a walk to the pond with Sonny in a day or two, when a hard hand seized her shoulder. She nearly fainted with fright. An angry face peered down at her, the face of an old man, weatherbeaten and tanned almost black. He had on a ragged pair of shorts and a T-shirt. His white hair was cropped very short, and on the back of his head he wore an old Navy watch cap. He was talking very fast, but Margaret was too frightened to get a word of what he was saying. She tried to pull away from him, but his hand gripped her shoulder like a vise.

Then abruptly he let go of her and stalked off to the other side of the beach, talking furiously to himself. Her impulse was to run, but he was paying no attention to her now, and she was curious about what he was doing. He had a pail and a big grocery bag with him.

She moved away from the beach, up the slope that led to the path, and there she waited to see what he was up to. She was still shaken by the sudden attack.

The old man picked up a big stick and pounded it on the sand. He really must be crazy, Margaret thought; he was still talking, but he didn't even look at her. He was staring toward the tall grass in the pond, where the log was.

Suddenly the log moved. Margaret gasped. It wasn't a log at all; it was the alligator. She was glad she hadn't decided to step on it. The alligator swam out to the middle of the pond, turned, and headed straight for the old man. Could alligators hear? The man was still pounding the stick on the ground and calling. Maybe the alligator felt the vibrations.

Whatever it was, it swam into the shallow water where the old man was and stopped. The man began pulling fish out of the pail and tossing them to the alligator. Sometimes the alligator caught the fish in its mouth, sometimes it missed and had to turn aside to find it. The man's hand was very close to the alligator's mouth, but he snatched it back each time just before the alligator reached for the fish.

After a few minutes he got a bag from the grocery sack and started throwing small white things at the alligator. Margaret couldn't make out what they were. They looked like marshmallows, but that was impossible. Fascinated, she forgot to be frightened and moved a little closer. They *were* marshmallows. And the alligator carefully retrieved them all and swallowed them.

When the fish and the marshmallows were gone, the man fed chunks of bread to the ducks. He looked up and saw her, and now he didn't look angry at all. He pointed to one of the ducks.

The duck was trailing one wing in the water.

Margaret decided to risk speaking. "How?"

"Kids." He started to get angry again, talking furi-

(*128*)

ously for a moment, too fast for her to catch, then he raised his hands in imitation of an aimed gun.

When he went back to feeding the ducks, he forgot her again. The alligator swam back to his position in the tall grass. Margaret stayed and watched until the old man gathered up his pail and his empty bags and strode off. She wondered if Josie knew who he was.

As she started home, she began to worry about those kids with guns. She shouldn't have left Sonny alone so long. She began to run. It seemed twice as far going back. She was running so heedlessly that at one turn in the path she crashed into a palm tree and scratched herself on the rough bark.

She called "Sonny" as soon as she came within sight of the boat. As far as she could tell, everything was as she had left it. She shinnied up the pine tree, dropped onto the deck, and ran to the deer. He looked up sleepily, chewing his cud. She flung her arms around him and held him tight.

17

JOSIE BROUGHT HOME SOME BOOKS: A BOOK ABOUT SEA birds, a secondhand copy of *Wuthering Heights* stamped with the name of a school library, a new Agatha Christie paperback, Rachel Carson's *The Edge of the Sea*, and a book called *Your Deafness Is Not You*, by Grace E. Barton Murphy. Margaret looked at them eagerly. The book on deafness caught her attention, and she looked at Josie.

Josie wrote: "Stopped to see a friend of mine. Eva Winship. Teaches biology. She lent us these."

Margaret wondered what Josie had told the friend about her. Why had Josie gone to see a teacher? But Josie went off to take her nap with no more explanations. Margaret took *Wuthering Heights* and the deafness book down to the beach. She started *Wuthering Heights*, but after a few pages she put it down and picked up the other book. Soon she was engrossed in the personal account of a woman whose deafness had come on early, as Margaret's had, and who had, like Margaret, loved and studied music.

It was low tide, but the remains of the storm she had hoped to pick up did not seem as important as the book. Kelp was everywhere, steaming in the sun, smelling strong, with clouds of little flies swarming around it. Sanderlings and sandpipers explored the beach, twinkling up and down the sand on their thin legs. Gulls swooped overhead. A foot-long, blue-green clam worm emerged from under a rock, looking like a miniature dragon, but Margaret hardly saw him. She was caught up in the astonishing story of this woman, who had endured so much suffering and hurt from being deaf yet had had such courage. The thing that moved Margaret most was the fact that the author never minimized the pain and the loss. Oh, yes, Margaret kept thinking, that's exactly how it is. It was almost dark when she finished the book. Her face was wet with tears she hadn't realized she'd shed. She felt drained but also good because here was someone else who knew what it was like.

When she finally went back on board, Josie was asleep, the binoculars on the deck beside her, the strap around her wrist. Margaret lay down beside Sonny and stared at the darkening sky, watching the stars come out.

Later, inside, Margaret tried to tell Josie about the book and about how it moved her.

Josie smiled. "Somebody who's been there and

knows." She repeated it. "There are lots of others, I expect."

"I guess so. I thought I didn't want to know any deaf people, but . . . I don't know . . ."

"It's nice to have you talking," Josie said. "Talking . . ." She flapped her fingers together.

Margaret said, "Will you tell me if my voice gets loud? I can't stand it if I start to yell at people."

"Yes." Josie wrote down: "Your voice a little hoarse now—you haven't talked lately and you're maybe tense. Just relax; you'll be fine."

In the morning after Josie had gone and the chores were done, Margaret took Sonny along the shore. He was putting some weight on his injured leg now, and Josie thought in a few days she might be able to take off the splint. "Youngsters' bones heal fast," she'd said.

Margaret was anxious for him to be all well, but she was worried, too. What if he went away and she never saw him again? Or, worse, what if she had to leave when Sonny left? Good sense told her that Josie wouldn't want her around forever. Till now she had always put the thought of leaving out of her mind, but she'd have to face it pretty soon. The thing to do was to ask Josie right out, but she doubted if she could bring herself to do that. Well, she still had the rest of Big Ed's money, and she could mail that letter to Becky and go back to her original plan. Only now it seemed almost too much to bear. She loved the life she was living, and Josie, Sonny, and the boat.

By early afternoon she had worried herself into feeling sleepy. She tied up Sonny and got him some leaves; then, leaving the machete on the deck, she curled up in Josie's hammock on the other side of the boat. She fell asleep, but it was an uneasy sleep. First the sun in her eyes woke her; then she moved too quickly and nearly fell out of the hammock. There was an art to sleeping in a hammock.

She had just drifted off to sleep again when something woke her. She didn't know what it was, but she was frightened. Disentangling herself from the hammock, she ran around the cabin to check on Sonny.

As she rounded the corner, she stopped short. Sonny was straining back against the bow rail, trembling all over, staring toward the gangplank. Just as Margaret turned her head to look, the big black dog broke loose from the woman who stood on the shore and hurled himself toward Sonny. Margaret jumped to grab him, but his rough coat slipped through her fingers. The dog leaped at Sonny, sinking his teeth into Sonny's shoulder.

Sonny tried to strike out with his forefeet, but he was hampered by the splint, which threw him off balance. He slipped and fell. But almost before he hit the deck, Margaret had both arms around the dog's middle, pulling him. The dog let go of Sonny and turned his head toward Margaret, snarling and showing his teeth. She hung on, trying to lift him clear of Sonny, but the dog was heavy. He sank his teeth into her wrist.

She lurched toward the rail, holding the dog; and exerting all her strength, she lifted him up and threw him overboard. He hit the water with a great splash.

Margaret grabbed the machete from the deck in case he tried to come back again after he got ashore. When she lifted her arm, she saw blood dripping from her wrist. The woman on shore had disappeared.

The dog floundered out of the water and took off, tail between legs and wet shaggy ears laid flat against his head.

Margaret went to take care of Sonny. The bite on his shoulder hadn't gone deep, but he was badly frightened. At first he wouldn't let Margaret touch him. She talked to him softly, just sitting near him and not trying to make him stand still. She wrapped a Kleenex around her own wound, but it was quickly soaked through.

When Sonny quieted down, she went below and washed her wrist with cold water and soap, and put two big Band-Aids on it. It didn't hurt much, but the dog had hit a small blood vessel or something, and it wouldn't stop bleeding. She took a bucket of water on deck and cleaned up the blood that had dripped from her hand.

Sonny twisted his head around so he could lick his cut. That would probably be the best way to take care of it. He began to relax, but when he heard Josie's bike coming along the path, he quivered all over again.

Josie listened, frowning, as Margaret told her what had happened. She looked at Margaret's wrist and said something sharp that Margaret didn't catch. Evidently she felt it needed more attention, because she got some gauze pads and some bandages and dressed the wound carefully.

"Lie down awhile," she said, pulling Margaret's sleeping bag over into the sunshine. "You're white as a ghost. Sonny's all right," she added, after she had looked at him. "Not a deep bite."

"He would have killed Sonny," Margaret said.

Josie nodded, her mouth set in a straight line. "I'll be right back," she said, and was gone before Margaret could say anything.

It was some time before she came back. Margaret had gotten up from her rest, had seen to Sonny, who was quiet now, and had gone below to see if there was anything she could do about dinner. Josie found her in the galley.

She got the pad. "No rabies shots needed."

Margaret was startled. She hadn't even thought of that.

"I talked to dogcatcher. Dog bit somebody last month. Tested him for rabies. Okay. Dog won't get loose again." Josie sat down at the table and opened a can of beer. "How does your wrist feel?" she said, tapping her own wrist.

"Oh, it just aches a little. Not bad."

"You scared Maisie Carter half to death."

"I had to."

Josie nodded. She sipped her beer thoughtfully and pulled the pad over. "Maisie doesn't know any better," she wrote. "She thinks you're a witch."

"Witch?"

Josie laughed and nodded.

"I thought *she* was," Margaret said.

18

TOWARD THE END OF THE WEEK, JOSIE CAME HOME ONE day and asked Margaret if she would help clean at the motel on Sunday. "Big crowd."

Margaret was startled. "Will I have to talk to people?" Then she added contritely, "Of course I'll help. I'll be glad to." After all Josie had done for her, she was ashamed of having hesitated the first time Josie asked a favor. "It will be fun," she added, hoping she sounded convincing.

But she worried about it all day Saturday. She hadn't had any experience with motels, but they always seemed to be full of people sitting around the pool with drinks in their hands, and lots of teenagers going off the diving board. But then, why worry about the pool? She was going to clean rooms. Or whatever Josie had in mind. Maybe she could dump trash and things like that.

Saturday night Margaret said, "Will Sonny be all right?"

Josie pointed to his splint. "Off tonight."

Margaret felt alarm. "He'll leave," she said. But inside the alarm was as much for herself as for Sonny. With him gone, was there any excuse for her staying?

"Can't keep him tied up, honey."

"I know. I just . . . had put off thinking about it."

After they had eaten, Josie took off Sonny's splint. He looked back at her in surprise. For a few moments he didn't touch his foot to the deck. Gently Josie took hold of it and helped him put it down. He shuddered and lifted it, but in a minute he tried again. She gave a little pull on his rope and he took a step, limping. Then more steps. With each one he limped less.

"It's psychological," Margaret said. "He thought it would hurt."

Josie handed the rope to Margaret. "Walk him." She crouched to watch Sonny's legs as Margaret led him up and down the deck, then stood up and nodded. "Just stiff." Pointing toward the shore, she indicated that Margaret should walk him there. Before they went down the gangplank, she took off the rope, but Sonny followed Margaret as if he still had the rope on.

Ashore, Margaret waited for Sonny to bound off into the brush, go off where she would never see him again. She thought she had prepared herself for losing him but now that it might happen any minute, she could hardly bear it.

Sonny, however, stayed close at her heels. He seemed bewildered at his new freedom, and a little anxious. She put her hand on his neck to reassure him. That kind of freedom was scary. You had to make your own decisions and strike out on your own. "Poor Sonny. You don't *have* to go. You can stay right here." The thought was comforting.

They walked along the shore in the swiftly falling darkness. On the way back Sonny made a few small excursions off the path, but in a few minutes he was back at her heels. And when Margaret went back aboard, he followed her. She felt immense relief. So far, nothing had really changed, except that Sonny had his choice.

When she got up early in the morning, he was in his old place, sleeping near the bow rail. She kissed the top of his head. Maybe he was going to be her own deer, forever. Maybe they would all be there together, forever.

She and Josie ate breakfast and started off for the motel, Josie wheeling the bike with its load of mops and brooms. Margaret asked Josie if the motel didn't let her use their cleaning things.

"I'm partial to my own," Josie said.

At the turn in the path Margaret looked back. Sonny stood on the deck watching them. It might be the last time she would ever see him. If she had a camera and could take a picture, some day she could say to her grandchildren, "Did I ever show you the picture of my pet Key deer?" Only she wouldn't ever have any grand-children.

She tried to think of anything but the motel as they walked up the sandy road. Josie talked to her, but she was too distracted to hear. Already the sun was hot and the air dense with humidity. All those people would be hanging around the pool. What if you knocked on a door, to clean, and the people were putting on their bathing suits or still in bed or something? She hoped she could just follow Josie around and help her.

They turned right at the highway and walked in the narrow path of coral and broken shells that bordered the road. Cars whizzed by, heading for Key West, and delivery trucks moved in both directions.

After a couple of minutes Josie turned in at a small motel. Margaret was surprised. She had expected the place to be big and elegant, like the motel where the dolphins were, but this place had only about twenty units. In the back there was a circular drive, with a clump of palm trees in the middle. Off at the right there were half a dozen big trash cans and a little utility shed. At the left of the circle was the pool, a rather small pool with some canvas chairs and a couple of small plastic tables. A short, blond man was cleaning palm fronds and scraps of paper out of the water with a long-handled scoop. He waved to Josie and smiled pleasantly at Margaret. No other people were in sight.

She stayed close at Josie's heels as Josie parked the bike, unlocked the door of the shed, wheeled the bike inside, and unloaded the cleaning utensils. Margaret tried to help, but she only whacked herself on the head with the mop handle. Her mother always said she was clumsy though she didn't really think she was, except when she was nervous.

Josie smiled at her encouragingly and gave her a big broom to carry. Margaret watched as Josie wheeled out a little cart and took it to a locked room. It was a small storage room, stacked high with clean towels, clean sheets, small cakes of soap, and packets of motel stationery. Josie worked fast, counting off the linens, towels, and the other things. The way she did it was very efficient, Margaret thought. She herself felt useless. She touched Josie's arm.

"What shall I do?"

Josie beckoned as she trundled the cart out of the storage room. She pointed to the vacuum cleaner standing outside the shed, and headed off toward the front of the motel. She walked briskly, with her head high, the way she always did, and Margaret saw that she was whistling. Hastily Margaret followed her, carrying the mop and the vacuum cleaner. It would take some hustling to keep up with Josie.

A woman lounged in the doorway of one of the units, in her bathrobe, drinking a cup of coffee from a plastic cup. Margaret saw Josie's head bob in greeting, but Josie didn't linger to see if she got a response. She got none, except a long, bored look from the woman. Margaret felt resentment on Josie's behalf. How dare these lazy, good-for-nothing drones snub a woman like Josie? But on the heels of that thought, she had another: Josie wouldn't care.

The people in the first unit had already checked out. Probably good people, Margaret thought, laughing at herself for carrying her grandfather's notion that an early riser was a virtuous person. She followed Josie into the room and changed her mind a little. They might be early risers, but they certainly had messy habits. Newspapers, cigarette butts, empty beer bottles, crumpled sacks from the hamburger place, dirty towels . . . the place was a shambles.

Josie looked at Margaret's wrinkled nose and laughed. "Par for the course," she said. She asked Margaret to dump the overflowing trash baskets in the big ones out by the shed. Eager to help, Margaret took all three baskets at once. They smelled of burned-out cigarettes, stale beer, rotting remains of sandwiches. People, she thought, should learn to be neater. After all, we all live on this earth.

She and Josie soon worked out a system for cleaning the rooms. Margaret stripped the beds, Josie made them up. Margaret emptied the trash, Josie did the bathrooms. Margaret swept, and Josie vacuumed. It was fun. Margaret had to work out a little method, doing everything in order so it would come out right. Josie smiled her approval.

On one of her trips back from the trash cans, Margaret stopped for a second to watch a boy do a fancy dive off the board. There were half a dozen older children in the pool, and one tall, thin man stretched out on his stomach on a canvas pad, his back reddening in the sun. The boy hit the pool just inches away from one of the girls. She shrieked and splashed toward the edge of the pool. The boy came up grinning, water streaming down his face. He followed the girl, making big waves with his arms. She burst into tears and left the pool.

By noon all the rooms were done except two that had DO NOT DISTURB signs on the door. Josie got Margaret a Seven-Up from the machine near the pool, and she herself got a cup of coffee in the office. She introduced Margaret to the woman at the reservations desk, who gave Margaret a friendly nod and said something that Margaret couldn't get at all. Later she remembered that Josie had said the people were French Canadian.

Embarrassed because she couldn't understand the woman, Margaret wandered out of the office, back toward the pool. There were only three children left there; the big boy who had done the diving, a skinny little boy, about eight or nine, and a slightly older girl who looked like him. The two younger children were swimming back and forth across the short side of the pool, dog paddling. The boy practiced his diving, ignoring the others. Margaret sat down in one of the canvas chairs and drank her Seven-Up.

One of the dives went wrong, and the boy landed in a belly flop, soaking Margaret. He made no acknowledgement. She got up and moved her chair back.

He dove again and swam the length of the pool, in a fast crawl, ignoring the two children, who thrashed desperately to get out of his way.

A pretty girl with long red hair came out of one of the rooms and flopped into the deck chair near Margaret. She watched the boy, and out of the corner of his eyes he watched her. He began to show off, doing fancy dives, and swimming very fast up and down the pool. She laughed when the two young children scrambled out of the water to get out of his way. The girl said something to Margaret, but she didn't catch it. She began to feel uneasy. It might be best to go back to Josie. But Josie was still in the office, talking to the owner. Margaret closed her eyes and pretended to be sunbathing.

After a few minutes she felt the Seven-Up bottle being snatched out of her hand. Startled, she looked up. The boy stood in front of her, grinning, and glancing continuously at the redheaded girl, who was laughing. Bewildered, Margaret looked from one to the other. The boy was talking and laughing, but she couldn't understand a word he said.

He pointed to a sign across the pool. Margaret read it. SWIMMING FOR GUESTS ONLY. PLEASE WEAR CAPS. PUT AWAY CHAIRS IN CASE OF WIND. NO BOTTLES NEAR POOL. No bottles. There were always so many rules about everything. She got up and held her hand out for the bottle. He held it out of reach and asked her something. She reached for the bottle, and he tossed it around her to the girl, who was standing just behind Margaret, laughing. Margaret began to get angry. If they dropped the bottle and broke it, she would get into trouble, and that meant trouble for Josie. She tried to take the bottle from the girl, but the boy darted around Margaret and got it from the girl. Margaret turned her back and started to walk away.

The boy caught her arm and held the bottle in the other hand, beyond her reach. The girl stood behind him, on the edge of the pool, in her crisp lime-colored shorts, her frilly yellow blouse, and her beautiful red hair.

Rage and frustration exploded in Margaret. Forgetting to consider the volume of her voice, she said, "Let go of me!" She saw their surprise, and in the instant of advantage that it gave her, she jerked loose from the boy's hold. The jerk threw him off balance. He stumbled backward against the red-haired girl. She flailed wildly for a moment and then fell backward into the pool. The boy dove in after her, the bottle still in his hand.

Margaret turned and saw the owner and Josie coming toward the pool. She ran.

When she got back to the boat, Sonny was gone. Margaret threw herself down on her sleeping bag, her despair too great for tears. Everything was ruined. She had ruined it herself. She would have to leave.

She was asleep when Josie got home. When she woke up, Josie was sitting in her deck chair, looking out at the

Gulf. Margaret waited nervously until Josie turned around. Josie smiled.

Margaret felt tears choke her throat. "Did you get fired?"

Josie laughed. "No way. Maids are scarce."

"I didn't mean to get you into trouble."

"You didn't. Let's go for a swim." She made a swimming motion.

Margaret wasn't sure whether Josie had said that, or whether she was referring to the incident at the pool. "I didn't mean for her to fall in . . ." She started to tell the story, but she knew her voice was getting loud and hoarse; she could feel it.

Josie came over and sat beside her on the deck. "No problem, Skipper."

But Margaret wanted to tell it all. She explained about the bottle, and about not seeing the sign. "I could at least have noticed the sign," she said bitterly. "I may be deaf, but I'm not blind." Josie tried to stop her, but then she let her go on and finish the story.

Josie got the pad and wrote something down. She showed it to Margaret. "Girl mad at boy; girl's mother mad at girl; boy too scared to be mad at anybody. *Nobody* mad at you."

Margaret could hardly believe it. Maybe Josie was just trying to make her feel good. "What about the owner?"

"She laughed." Josie pulled some bills out of her pocket. "Your pay."

Margaret shook her head. "I can't take money. I almost lost you your job. Just because I couldn't hear. . . . I should go away . . . too much trouble." Tears filled her eyes and she turned her head away.

Josie handed her the pad of paper. She had written: "It would probably have been just the same if you had heard them. It was nothing, Skipper. Don't be dramatic about your deafness."

Margaret was shocked. Josie had never said anything sharp or unkind. She looked up at her in disbelief. Josie laughed and gave her a quick hug. "Come swim. You'll feel better. And no more of that talk about leaving."

Of course she did feel better after the swim, but it wasn't the kind of feeling better you could trust. It was just that the water was cool, and when you swam out a way, you got the feeling the world wasn't there anymore—the people part of the world—and that was reassuring. It was nice to know, too, that Josie really wanted her. But that didn't solve her real problem. She saw that now.

She tried to tell this to Josie. Josie listened intently, frowning a little, whether in concentration or disapproval, Margaret didn't know.

After a while Josie reached for the pad, which she did when she wanted to be sure Margaret understood her. "Skipper, I think you need more people, not fewer."

Margaret shook her head. Not even Josie understood

how hard it was. "They just make fun of me," she said. "Those kids at the pool . . ."

Josie interrupted her with a gesture and wrote rapidly. "They didn't know you were deaf. It had nothing to do with that." She hesitated and then wrote some more. "People are kinder than you think. You just have to learn to deal with them in a different way now." She paused again. "You can't hide, Skipper."

Margaret felt betrayed. Josie didn't understand; no normal person could. Wearily she said, "All right," and went ashore to look for Sonny. Not that she expected to find him.

19

MONDAY EVENING WHEN JOSIE AND MARGARET CAME
up on deck after dinner, Sonny was in his usual place
by the bow rail, chewing his cud, as if he had never
been away. He looked at Margaret with calm eyes as
she ran up to him.

"I thought you were gone for good." She was almost
in tears, she was so glad to see him. "Look, Josie, doesn't
he look grown up!"

"Looks fine." Josie patted his neck, and he reached
his head around and gently caught her fingers in his
mouth. She laughed. "Good old Sonny."

Margaret saw Sonny turn his head alertly toward the
other end of the boat, and at the same time Josie looked
back. It flashed across Margaret's mind that it was the
woman with the dog. That woman had taken on the
aspect of a witch in Margaret's mind; she often found
herself looking nervously over her shoulder as she

walked along the shore, expecting to see that hulking figure following her.

But it was not the woman. It was a young policeman. Margaret felt cold in her stomach. She was sure he had come about her; about the girl getting dumped in the pool. Could they arrest you for a thing like that? It had been an accident, after all . . .

Josie was greeting the policeman with a big smile. Shaking hands, even. They were talking, but their faces were turned away from her. Anyway she was too nervous ever to have followed what they were saying. Her head rang and buzzed with the racket that always increased when she was upset. This was it: this was the thing that Josie and everybody failed to understand: she had lost all control over events. Things went on that might or might not affect her whole life, or even just a tiny moment of her life, and she had no way at all of knowing what those things were, or what was going on, until someone remembered to clue her in. Even then, she just got the bare essentials, and lots of times it was the little things that were most important, a tone of voice, an apparently casual comment; these were the things she never got. In a spasm of frustration she turned her back on Josie and the cop and gripped the boat rail with both hands. Off the end of the peninsula a pelican seemed by sheer will power to propel his ungainly body along, just above the green water. Plop! He dove heavily for his supper.

She started, as Josie touched her shoulder. The policeman smiled at her pleasantly as Josie introduced them. He said something, but Margaret didn't get it. She was thinking he couldn't really arrest her because she was a minor; and he couldn't make her tell who her mother was. But Josie would get in trouble for harboring a delinquent. Any way you turned, there was a roadblock.

The cop was patting Sonny, who shrank away from the strange touch. Margaret looked at the man's arm patch again to make sure he wasn't Fish and Game. No, he was just a plain cop.

He smiled again at Margaret and walked slowly back along the deck with Josie. Smiles, smiles. People smiled too much, and it meant nothing. She watched the cop shake hands with Josie and leave the boat.

Josie came back and sat down beside Margaret. "Friend of Danny's," she said. "Known him since . . ." She measured about a foot in height.

Margaret wanted to feel relieved. Friend of Danny's; social call. But she didn't really believe that was it. There was something else in Josie's face, a faraway look, a worried look.

Josie sat quite still for several minutes, watching the sky. Finally she said, "He came about you."

Well, if things happened, they happened, and you just had to cope the best way you could. She would never tell her real name, and she would swear Josie just let her stay on the boat out of kindness. They didn't put people in jail or fire them from their jobs for plain old human kindness, did they?

"About the girl that fell in the pool?" She asked not because she needed to be told, but because she wanted to help Josie break the news.

Josie looked surprised. "No, no. About school."

"What?"

"Somebody told them you were here."

"Who?" But she was sure she knew who. That teacher. Miss Winship. All teachers could think about was getting you into a school.

Josie brushed off the question. "Who knows." She nodded at Margaret reassuringly. "Let me sleep on it. I'll think of something."

Obviously, Josie didn't understand that there was nothing anyone could do with a deaf kid but send her to a school for the handicapped. And Margaret had made up her mind about that. That night after Josie was asleep in her hammock, Margaret went quietly below and began to pack.

It didn't take long because she didn't have much. She could have done it in the morning, but if she waited, she might weaken and try to talk herself into thinking it would be all right to stay. This way she could go off like a shot as soon as Josie left.

She stacked up the books. She wished she could take them, especially that good one by the deaf woman, but they belonged to the school. Maybe when she got to Maine, she could find it in the library. She thought about her grandfather's house, big, cold, and drafty; and for a moment she despaired of being able to live in it alone.

Even if they let her. Somebody would catch up with her, just the way they had here. But if she didn't go to Maine, where could she go? There didn't seem to be any place for her in the whole world. She leaned her head against the wall and began to cry.

She jumped at a light touch on her back. It was Josie, hair rumpled, eyes sleepy. She beckoned Margaret into the galley. "Cocoa?" Without waiting for an answer, she began to get out the milk. Margaret was ashamed of having been found in tears, but Josie seemed not to notice.

"Sonny's gallivanting again," Josie said. She had to repeat the word "gallivanting," and Margaret laughed. It was a word her grandfather had used about women, "always gallivanting around, drinking tea and crucifying their neighbors," he'd say. But he didn't mean it. He liked to grumble. Margaret understood that better now; the little conversations and distractions that most people used to keep their minds off their troubles were closed to the deaf, so it was easier for the deaf to brood and get depressed. That was why Grandfather grumbled and sputtered, to keep his mind off his deafness.

Josie mistook Margaret's thoughtful expression for concern about Sonny. "He'll be back. You're his mama. He loves you."

"He doesn't need me now."

"I didn't say need; I said love. Two different things."

When the milk was hot and the cocoa made, Josie filled the big mugs and sat down. "Listen." She spoke extra slowly. "I've got an idea. Have to talk to someone first. But I think it will work."

"I'm not going to any handicapped school."

"Trust me. And don't go away." She wrote it down and underlined it. "DON'T GO."

Margaret nodded. She didn't see what plan Josie could have that would work, but if Josie said wait, she'd wait. She wanted to trust Josie.

"Promise?"

"I promise."

Josie put the empty mugs in the sink and rinsed them out. When she and Margaret were on deck, she patted Margaret's shoulder and said something, but it was too dark to see her lips.

Margaret lay on her back on her sleeping bag, staring up at the dense black sky with its silver blanket of stars. A full moon made a shifting path of light on the Gulf, and she lifted up on her elbow for a few minutes to watch it. She tried to think what it would feel like to be weightless. Sometimes she wished she were thoughtless, too. Just enough mind to be conscious of physical sensations, the cool water and the pleasure of swimming, the touch of piano keys, things like that. She lay down again and closed her eyes.

Josie was gone when she awoke in the morning. A note on the galley table said, "Don't forget your promise. Saw Sonny hanging around. Love, *J*."

She took a papaya on deck and ate it slowly. Josie

said the Conchs usually cooked papayas and guavas, but Margaret liked them raw.

After a while she went ashore to look for Sonny, but she couldn't find him. She had the feeling he might be watching her hunt for him, playing a game with her, but although she turned sharply several times, she never caught a glimpse. She stopped to look at a little bird with white bars on his wings and what looked like white eyeglasses. His white throat swelled with singing. She wished, if she couldn't hear him, that she could at least touch that vibrating throat. She took a step toward him, and he flew away.

She had never walked this far along the shore before. If she hadn't promised Josie, she would be tempted to keep on going until she came out somewhere, or never came out; she could live in the forest like Rima the Bird Girl, live on fruit and fish . . .

She followed a faint, heavily overgrown path out onto the peninsula that they could see from the boat. Might as well walk around it. Palm fronds flapped in her face, and she thought of something she had read once about their ghostly rustle. She tripped over a mangrove root and almost fell. Her legs were scratched, and a cloud of tiny insects swarmed around her head. She made herself slow down. No sense blundering into a snake or something.

It was longer around the perimeter of the peninsula than she had expected but she plodded on, determined to go through with it. The air had grown heavy and wet; she felt as if she were swimming. Her face was streaming with perspiration and her shirt clung to her shoulder blades. It was stupid not to go back, but it had become some kind of test.

At the end of the peninsula, she had a clear view of the Gulf for a moment, before the path swung around to the other side. She was surprised to see how dark the sky had become. As she watched, lightning flashed. Probably it had been thundering, and as usual she didn't even know the most fundamental things that were going on, like weather. It would probably pour down rain in a minute, but that was all right; it would cool her off. She was soaking wet anyway. She shook her shoulders, annoyed by the drops of sweat that trickled down her back.

Three birds darted in front of her, at the level of her face, and the rain came. But it did not cool her. It was a hot rain, like a steam bath. She started back along the other side of the peninsula. Here the path was even fainter. Once she stopped short, sure she had seen the last slither of a snake out of the corner of her eye. She shuddered and waited, wondering why she had ever wandered into this dangerous jungle when she ought to be comfortably and safely on the boat, waiting for Josie's solution, Josie's plan. But she knew it was because she didn't believe in any plan that she was here, trying to forage for herself. Like Robinson Crusoe or somebody.

She stopped short. On the path in front of her, almost hidden by the curtain of rain, lay a dead raccoon. His head had been torn from his body, and the ground around him was reddish brown from blood. It seemed to Margaret just then to be one of the most awful things that could have happened. She prayed it was not the raccoon she had talked to from the boat. But whoever he was, it was awful. She knelt in the wet muck beside him, but she couldn't quite bring herself to touch him.

A movement off to the side of the path caught her eye. She turned and faced the big ugly dog, the dog that belonged to the big, ugly woman, the witch-woman. Her first reaction to the sight of him was fear, but quickly the fear gave way to rage. It seemed obvious that the dog had killed the raccoon, and now he was challenging her for the prey. Half menacing, half cringing, he faced her, his mouth open. She knew he was snarling. Behind him the rain slanted off the water of the Gulf, and all around them wind agitated the trees. Margaret yelled at the dog. He backed up, his lip pulled up over his yellow teeth. Then, when she did nothing, he advanced again, head lowered and threatening.

Margaret looked down at the torn body of the raccoon. In a gust of a fury she picked up a rock and threw it at the dog as hard as she could. It hit him over the eye. She saw his mouth open for a howl of pain, and she saw blood gush from the wound. She braced herself for his attack, but instead he took off up the trail, tail between his legs. He disappeared quickly in the rain and the vegetation. If she could only hear him, she would know where he was. But she would have to risk his jumping out at her if she moved up the trail.

She looked down at the raccoon. Already he looked like a muddy mass of fur and dirt, with only the head to show that he had been a beautiful, living, bright-eyed animal. Rage at the dog and helpless pity for the raccoon left her shaking.

There was no way to bury him here. Perhaps near the water . . . but it would just be coral and mangrove. As she stood there, a huge form rushed out of the rain toward her, lit up for an instant by a flash of lightning. It was the big ugly woman and she was in a fury, waving her arms and apparently yelling, her mouth open, showing gaps in her teeth. Margaret was faint with fear. She was sure the woman was going to beat her up for hitting the dog.

But the woman was pointing at the raccoon. Suddenly Margaret understood. The dog had hunted down the raccoon for the woman. Southern country people ate raccoon. As the woman came toward the raccoon, Margaret stooped and picked up the torn head and the muddy carcass. Without looking back at the woman, she crashed through the brush toward the Gulf. Although she could not hear her and didn't look back, she felt the woman close behind her. She plunged through a tangle of brush, tearing her jeans, and as she reached the water, she flung the raccoon's body and head out into the water. They struck a dark incoming wave. For a moment the head bobbed grotesquely on the surface, but then like the rest of the carcass it sank.

Margaret felt the woman's grasp on her arm. She flung her arm upward, breaking loose, and tried to run. But the rain blinded her and the brush caught at her feet like live hands. She tripped and fell forward into a patch of something prickly. She thought: The woman will kill me.

At the same moment that the thought flashed through her mind, she felt a pain, like a hot poker thrust into the palm of her hand. She jerked her hand back and saw a snake slip through the leaves and disappear. She screamed. The woman jerked her to her feet, and Margaret held out her hand. They both stared at the puncture wound. The woman said something. Roughly she picked Margaret up and carried her as if she were a baby, slung over her huge arm. When they got out of the brush, she lay Margaret down on her back on the path and Margaret saw the flash of a knife blade in the woman's hand. A wave of nausea struck her, and then as the woman seized her hand and brought the knife blade toward it, Margaret fainted.

20

THE WOMAN WAS CARRYING MARGARET SLUNG OVER HER
shoulder again. Margaret slipped in and out of con-
sciousness, burning with fever, nauseated, too sick to
be frightened any longer. It didn't matter now what
the woman did with her; Margaret had seen the dark
diamond pattern on the skin of the snake, and she was
sure she would die. She felt too sick even to be frightened by that.

She was vaguely aware of being put down on something soft. A cool cloth was put on her head. She opened
her eyes and looked up at a strange roof, but looking
made her dizzy, and she closed her eyes again.

The next time she woke, her fever had gone down.
She was in a cabin that she didn't recognize for a
moment. Then she remembered it; it was Josie's little
cabin. She half raised up, but the exertion made her feel
faint. Josie was not there, but the big woman stood in

the doorway, leaning against it, her back toward Margaret. She was smoking a cigar. Surprised to be in this cabin, surprised even to be alive, Margaret looked at her hand. It was wrapped in clean strips of bandage held together with tape.

The woman turned around and looked at her. Then she went outside. Now that she felt better, Margaret was worried about the woman again. And yet if anyone had helped her, it must have been the woman. She remembered now the gleam of the knife, and the quick pain, and later the sensation of being carried like a sack of oats. Maybe she had been awfully wrong about this woman. She'd been afraid of her because of the dog and because she looked so wild and waved her arms like a madwoman. Maybe people are scared of me sometimes, she thought, because I don't react the way they expect. Like those kids at the pool.

Josie came in, and Margaret forgot everything else, seeing her quick, happy walk. "Hi," Josie said, smiling. She put her hand on Margaret's forehead and then took her pulse. "Fine." She sat down on the edge of the bed. "How do you feel?"

"Kind of groggy, but a lot better. I got bitten by a rattlesnake."

"I know. Thank God for Maisie."

It went through Margaret's mind that if it hadn't been for Maisie, she wouldn't have gotten bitten in the first place. But that wasn't really fair. She had thrown away the woman's raccoon, probably her dinner . . . Thinking about it made her head ache. When you got into what caused what, it was always complicated.

"How did I end up here?"

"She brought you here and came for me. The doctor . . ." She said it again. "Doctor came. Said you're okay."

"Doctor? I don't remember."

"You were sleeping."

"When can I go home?"

"Tomorrow."

"Will you be here tonight?" In spite of herself Margaret glanced toward the woman who hulked in the doorway.

Josie nodded. "Get some sleep now."

In the afternoon of the next day, Josie took Margaret back to the boat. It was good to get back. She still felt weak, and she lay on the deck in the quiet sunshine, sometimes thinking, sometimes just lying there, swaying gently in Josie's hammock.

After several days of this pleasant laziness, Josie came home one afternoon with someone else. A woman, small and slender, with vivid blue eyes and short, curly gray hair. It was Eva Winship. Margaret could hardly believe it. She had expected a big, formidable woman with a schoolteachery scowl. This small, attractive Miss Winship limped a little, but it didn't slow her down any.

Josie introduced them and went below to get iced tea. Miss Winship sat down in Josie's chair and looked at Margaret with bright, interested eyes.

"Where's Sonny?"

Margaret was surprised that she even knew about Sonny. "He's gallivanting around on shore somewhere."

"How's his leg?"

Miss Winship sat facing the sun and she spoke distinctly. She was easy to lip-read.

"Better. He hardly limps at all now." Immediately she was embarrassed at having mentioned limping.

But Miss Winship nodded matter-of-factly. "Good. It slows a person down. What grade were you in?"

The change of subject took Margaret by surprise, and she had to ask Miss Winship to repeat the question. "I was nearly through the eighth." She wanted to add "why?" Her suspicions were aroused again. School was in the air. She missed Miss Winship's next remark altogether, but just then Josie came up with the pitcher of iced tea.

Margaret gave Josie her chair, and she sat on the deck, not even trying to follow the conversation. After a while Miss Winship leaned forward and asked to see the mark of the snakebite. Margaret showed it to her.

"I'm deathly afraid of snakes," she said. "I'd have fainted dead away."

"I did," Margaret said.

Josie said, "Thank God for Maisie Carter."

Miss Winship said slowly, "I want to tell you about something. Will you stop me if you don't understand?"

Margaret nodded. Here it came, whatever it was.

Speaking slowly and distinctly and repeating key

words, Miss Winship told her she had a friend at the university in Coral Gables who conducted a workshop for the profoundly deaf.

Margaret tensed, and Josie said quickly, "Not a live-in school, Skipper. You could stay with me."

Miss Winship found some paper and wrote out some of what she wanted to say. Her friend, she wrote, combined speech reading, natural sign language, and any other method of communication he could use, and his idea was to train people so they could take part in regular classes. There were some schools now, she wrote, that combined special classes with regular classes.

Margaret studied their faces. "It's too far away."

"I'll get a job in Miami," Josie said. "We'll come to the boat weekends."

"It's not a terribly long course," Miss Winship said. "Well, not really a course at all. A workshop. Workshop."

Josie patted her arm. "Think about it." She got up and refilled the iced tea glasses, and she and Miss Winship talked of other things.

Margaret sat looking out over the water, her knees pulled up under her. She wanted to say no. She dreaded any new situation, especially one that directly involved her deafness. And yet she'd known all along that she couldn't just sit there on Josie's boat till she was an old lady ready to die. Her grandfather used to talk about "fighting your way out of a paper bag." That's how she felt, only the bag was something a lot more restricting than paper. The thing that touched her, impressed her, was that Josie was willing to change her whole life, leave her beloved boat five days out of the week for who knew how long, just so Margaret could go to this school that wasn't a school. She guessed she owed it to Josie to give it a try. She sighed.

When Miss Winship was leaving, Margaret said, "Will it cost a lot?"

Miss Winship shook her head. "Nothing."

"Okay. I'd like to try it." It was hard to say it. But the look that lit up Josie's face made her glad she had.

Miss Winship gave them a cheerful nod and limped down the gangplank and off the path faster than most people walk.

Josie smiled and shook her head. "She's a wonder." She beamed at Margaret. "Now we'll lick 'em."

"Sure," Margaret said. She hoped her misgivings didn't show. Yet, there was always the chance that it would turn out okay. It might even be the way out she had been looking for. She smiled back at Josie. Better something than nothing.

21

"I'D BETTER LET MY MOTHER KNOW," MARGARET SAID.

Things had moved fast. Miss Winship had made arrangements with the man at the university; Josie's boss at the motel had helped her find a five-day-a-week job with a janitorial service; and the man at the university had found rooms for them near the campus.

It was time to tell her mother where she was. There wouldn't be any problem, now that she had been taken care of. Her mother would be relieved, and she wouldn't have to bother with her conscience.

Josie didn't ask any questions about this mother she had not heard of before. She only said, "Do you want me to call her or will you write?"

Margaret knew she had to write. Her mother would have a fit if some stranger called her up about her child. She'd take it as a criticism. She went below and found some paper. Briefly she told her mother where she was and what she planned to do.

I know it'll be a big load off your mind to know I'm okay and all. Hope you're having a fine time with your husband.

Affectionately,
Margaret

She sealed the envelope.

Now that it was written, she was anxious to mail the letter right away. She told Josie she was going to the store to mail it. And she had something else on her mind. She had worried about doing Maisie Carter out of her dinner, that raccoon that would have gone into a stew or something. After she mailed her letter, she went into the grocery store and bought a big T-bone steak. It was expensive. She hoped it was a delicacy that Mrs. Carter couldn't afford, so it would not only make up for the raccoon but for saving her life too. Not that it could really make up for that, of course . . . What she really wanted, she thought, was to make amends for having thought badly of Mrs. Carter. She was going to try not to misjudge people in the future.

As she turned off into the overgrown path that led to Mrs. Carter's shack, she began to feel nervous. She hoped the woman would take the gift as she meant it and not feel insulted. In Maine people were apt to feel insulted if you gave them something. She almost lost her nerve; she could take the steak home to Josie. But then she saw the face of the dog through the trees, his mouth open; she could tell he was barking. She inched along the path until she could see the shack. The dog was chained to a tree. Mrs. Carter came out onto the rickety porch, flapping her big dirty white apron to drive off the flies. Smoke was coming out of the skinny little chimney. She saw Margaret and stood still, staring at her.

Margaret had worked up in her mind an image of Mrs. Carter as a diamond in the rough, a simple but kindly soul who had gone to great trouble to save her from a nasty death. But she looked in vain for that image. Mrs. Carter looked just as wild-eyed, just as unfriendly, as ever; her uncombed hair streamed from her head like wires, and her expression made her look like a snarling dog that might charge at any moment. Margaret's impulse was to run, but having come this far, she decided to finish it. Skirting the dog, she went up to Mrs. Carter, who didn't move, and held out the package of steak.

"Thank you for saving my life. And I'm sorry about the raccoon." She could tell she had spoken in a loud, strained voice. Mrs. Carter took a step backward and made no move to take the meat. Margaret laid it on the step and went back down the path, making an effort not to run. Just before she got back to the boat, she remembered that the woman had very few teeth. The steak would probably be tossed into a stew, or given to that awful dog. She had made her gesture, but it didn't make her feel as good as she had thought it would. Maybe you just couldn't cancel out a bad deed with a good one. It didn't seem fair, though, if you couldn't be sorry and be forgiven and forget it.

Later she told Josie what she had done.

"Nice thought," Josie said. But she didn't carry on about it the way Margaret hoped she would.

"She didn't even smile."

"Maisie never smiles. Never had much to smile about."

"She didn't even say thank you."

Josie looked at Margaret a minute. Then she took out the pad of paper. "Don't expect State-of-Maine tea parties from somebody like Maisie." She showed it to Margaret. Then she added: "She will enjoy the steak. Never mind about gratitude." Josie was smiling, but Margaret took it as a rebuke, and she felt hurt.

It wasn't until she was swimming, a few days later, that she finally admitted to herself that Josie was right. If you gave somebody something, you shouldn't worry about being thanked. Especially if the gift was a kind of making up for something. And for all Mrs. Carter knew, that package might have been a big firecracker or something mean. Margaret had never given her any reason to expect a friendly gift.

As she turned to swim back, she thought of something she had read, either in the book by the deaf woman or somewhere else: The deaf brood too much. Right. She'd have to watch that.

She swam in a wide half circle, looking over at the

shore whenever her head came out of the water. It had been days since she had seen Sonny. She kept looking for him, but she was losing hope. He'd probably gone off to some other part of the Key.

She turned over on her back and floated, squinting up at the bright sky. She went over in her mind a newspaper clipping that Miss Winship had sent her by Josie. It was about a new discovery that might cure her kind of deafness. A little gimmick recharged the hearing nerves, like recharging a battery. In tests it had been fifty percent effective. Fifty percent. Well, it was something to think about. Life was beginning to seem like a slot machine or something; if you had a fifty-fifty chance, that was probably pretty good. She wondered what the odds would be on her drowning before she got back to the boat.

She turned over and saw a strange-looking sea creature a few feet away from her, part of it above water. It was beautiful, bright yellow, orange, and red, with a lot of little fluttering tentacles. It looked like the pompons girls wore at football games, only prettier. She stayed still, treading water, to watch it. She wondered if it was poisonous.

Finally, she turned and swam toward the boat. It must be about time for Josie. She hung for a moment on the rope ladder, hating to get out of the cool water. Her eyelashes stuck together, and there was a taste of salt on her tongue. She looked up at a gull circling overhead. Then she gripped the rope and climbed to the deck.

Josie was standing near the cabin, her back to Margaret, and two people were coming up the gangplank. Margaret's mother and Big Ed. Margaret stood staring at them, water dripping from her bathing suit in a little puddle around her. Her mother was wearing a new yellow pantsuit that looked expensive. Ed had his hand on her arm.

"Margaret!" Her mother pulled away from Ed and started to run toward Margaret. She was wearing white wooden clogs, and she slipped. Ed jumped forward and caught her, but she pulled loose again and came to Margaret. "Margaret, for goodness' sake!" She started to hug Margaret but she noticed the wet bathing suit and thought better of it. "For the love of Mike, Margaret." It was one of her old slang expressions from her girlhood. Margaret laughed.

"Hi, Mother. How are you? You look great."

Her mother narrowed her eyes. "You're talking."

"Right." Margaret smiled at Josie. Her mother turned and looked at Josie suspiciously.

". . . worried sick."

Margaret got only the two words. As usual her mother talked too fast. And her own head buzzed like a swarm of locusts. Now that they had seen each other, she wished her mother would just go away, go on with her life. Her mother was speaking to Josie, and Josie answered, but Margaret didn't get any of it. Ed joined the conversation, with his same old foolish grin.

(*174*)

". . . scared to death," Margaret's mother said to her accusingly.

"I'm sorry you worried. I told you I'd be all right." Margaret caught Josie's warning gesture and lowered her voice. "I'm going to this class at the university . . ."

Her mother was talking a blue streak, and her face was flushed. Margaret caught a few words: ". . . my responsibility . . . school in St. Augustine . . ." Then she turned back to Josie, and Margaret couldn't get any of it. Josie was talking and smiling, but she looked strained. Margaret wanted to scream with frustration. They couldn't talk about her like this, as if she were a T-bone steak and they were fighting over who was going to get it . . . She grabbed her mother's arm.

"Listen. It's all settled. I'm accepted by this professor. He can teach me to get along better than anybody can, almost like normal . . ." She began to cry, but she kept on talking. "You did all you could. Nobody can blame you. Now let me have a chance. I won't go to that school in St. Augustine, or any other handicapped school. I'll kill myself first."

Now her mother began to cry. Big Ed looked distressed. Margaret saw Josie speak to him, and then the two of them went below. Her mother didn't notice. She was weeping and reciting her woes, back to Grandfather and the aunts and her own first marriage.

"All right," Margaret said. "All right, that's all over now. Forget it. Enjoy yourself." She looked at her mother's face, the makeup smeared with tears, and she felt sudden pity. "Oh, Mama," she said, in a quiet voice, "don't tear yourself apart. You've got Ed. Enjoy it."

"All my life. . . ." The tears flowed again.

Margaret's moment of pity disappeared in exasperation. "You're not dead yet. Why don't you enjoy the rest of your life? Maine is a million miles away. And now you don't even have to worry about me."

"A stranger . . ." her mother said.

"She may be a stranger to you, Mother, but she's the best friend I've ever had." But that was the wrong thing to say. There was another burst of tears and words.

Then Ed and Josie came on deck, Ed carrying the pitcher of iced tea, Josie the glasses. Ed put his big arm around Margaret's mother and murmured to her. She took his handkerchief and dabbed at her face. Ed got her to sit down, and Josie poured them all tea.

Margaret had never been able to understand Ed at all, and she couldn't now. She sat on the deck and watched, her own glass of tea untouched, as Ed talked earnestly to her mother. Josie kept tactfully out of the way.

Margaret's mother was listening to Ed. Once she looked at Margaret, and Margaret caught the word "handicapped." It was a word she hated. She interrupted. "Other people have things. They're lame or blind or they have heart trouble or something. So what? They don't have to crawl off in a corner and die. Pretty soon people just take them the way they are." She caught Josie's signal that meant "Don't talk." She turned away and stared angrily out at the Gulf. They would take her away and dump her in some awful school, just to satisfy her mother's kooky conscience, just so she could say, "I had my cross to bear and I bore it." You couldn't win when somebody was bound and determined to be a martyr.

Big Ed was talking up a storm. Margaret's mother got up and stood by the taffrail, not looking at Ed but listening. Margaret marveled that there was someone at last who could make her mother be quiet and listen.

Suddenly Margaret's mother turned and said impatiently, "All right, all right." She came over to Margaret. "Go ahead. But I want a report once a month. You hear me?"

Margaret nodded. The relief was so great, she thought she would fall over. So unexpected . . . "Yes, Mother. Once a month."

Her mother turned to Josie and talked hard and fast, frowning. Josie listened and nodded. Big Ed shook hands with Josie. Margaret's mother did not. She gave Margaret a kiss on the cheek, her eyes filled with tears once more, and she marched off the boat. Ed aimed a kiss at the top of Margaret's head and missed. He grinned and said something, shook hands with Josie again, and followed his wife. Margaret watched them out of sight. Ed turned once and waved, but her mother never turned. It was always hard for her mother to give in.

Margaret flopped down in a deck chair and looked at Josie. "What happened?"

Josie laughed. "Your mother's husband said I had a shipshape boat."

"A what?"

Josie pointed to the boat. "Shipshape."

"What did that have to do with anything?"

"If I can manage the boat, I can manage you."

Margaret thought about it and then laughed. "He's right." She began to shiver. Josie got her a towel. "Is it all right, then? I can go to the university?"

"Yes."

Margaret marveled. "My mother almost never gives in."

"Perhaps she wants to, sometimes." Josie pulled a piece of paper from her pocket and showed it to Margaret. It was Ed's check for $500. "I didn't want it, but that was his price. He pays."

Margaret was glad Ed had done that. Now she wouldn't have to worry about imposing on Josie. "Good. I'm glad."

"Bank," Josie said. "College."

Well, they could settle that later. Margaret snuggled up in the towel, feeling almost weak with contentment. She thought she would get dressed and write to Becky, now that she had something to talk about.

Josie got out the binoculars and scanned the shore. "I saw Sonny this morning."

Margaret sat up eagerly. "Sonny? Where?"

Josie pointed to a place down the shore. "He was watching the boat."

"I thought he'd gone forever."

She shook her head. "He'll stick around." She handed the glasses to Margaret. There was no sign of a deer anywhere along the shore now. But it made her happy to know he was around and safe.

Later she started her letter to Becky, sitting in a deck chair and using a magazine for a desk.

Dear Becky,

I guess you're surprised to hear from me at last. You must think I've gone to the moon or something. I wrote once but it never got mailed. This is neat country, really neat. My mother got married, as you may know by now, and I'm living with a friend on the neatest *houseboat*. I'm going to be a Research Subject in a project for the deaf at the University of Miami. Boy, am I important . . . ha ha. I'm going to learn how to go to regular school again, if all goes well.

She picked up the binoculars and looked at the shore. No Sonny yet.

Hey, Beck, I've got my own pet fawn. His name is Sonny and he's very small, what is called a Key deer. I sort of saved his life. Also I was bitten by a rattlesnake, but as I guess you can tell, I survived. If you ever come to Florida, Beck, look me up, don't forget. I may get up to Maine some day but not for a while. Say hi to everybody. Write.

Love,
Margaret

The picture of her mother walking up the path so fast, her shoulders hunched, came into her mind. It was hard for her mother to lose an argument. It always had been. Tonight she'd write her a friendly letter and thank her for all she'd done.

Josie came on deck with a big plate of hot bollos. She pulled up her own chair, and they sat lazily in the sun, eating the bollos and watching the big seabirds out on the Gulf. Somewhere along the shore, hidden in a camouflage of trees and brush, Sonny was probably chewing away on silver palm leaves.